Praise for Irene Ha

"A warmhearted journey from loss and guilt to self-forgiveness and love."

—*Romantic Times Book Reviews* on *Once Upon Nantucket*

"Complex characters, wonderful seaside setting, and a heartwarming plot make this story hard to put down."

—*Goodreads* review on *The Hero Next Door*

"The setting is perfect, the characters are complex and endearing, making this story a heartwarming journey. Hard to say goodbye."

—*Goodreads* review on *Meant for Each Other*

"A wonderful story of forgiveness and healing and second chances...and don't we all need to be swept away in this day and time to be reminded how great it is to love and be loved. You can't go wrong with a book from Irene Hannon."

—*Amazon* review on *A Father for Zach*

"Inspiring prose and embraceable characters...capture the reader from the very first pages."

—*New York Journal of Books* on *That Certain Summer*

"Hannon's multithread plot is woven beautifully together to create a tapestry that will enchant romantics of all ages."

—*Publishers Weekly* on *One Perfect Spring*

"A great summer read...relatable characters with real-life problems."

—*Radiant Lit* on *Seaside Reunion*

"Hannon has such a gift for storytelling. Measured words, taut pacing, endearing characters, and plot twists abounding! I've enjoyed everything I've read by this gifted author."

—**Best Reads 2010-2019** on *Finding Home*

"We all make mistakes…but they don't need to burden us forever. And sometimes we get a second chance to make things right. Friendly faces and stunning scenery await…just right for a summer read."

—**Fresh Fiction** on *Only You*

Once Upon Nantucket

LIGHTHOUSE LANE—BOOK ONE
ENCORE EDITION

IRENE HANNON

©2009 by Irene Hannon

First edition published 2009 by Harlequin Love Inspired as *Tides of Hope*

Encore Edition published 2023 by Irene Hannon

(An Encore Edition is a previously published novel that has been re-edited and reissued with a new cover.)

All rights reserved. No part of this publication may be reproduced, stored in a retrieval system, or transmitted in any form or by any means—for example, electronic, photocopy, recording—without the prior written permission of the author. The only exception is brief quotations in printed reviews.

ISBN 9781970116144

This book is a work of fiction. Names, characters, places, and incidents are the product of the author's imagination or are used fictitiously. Any resemblance to actual events, locales, or persons, living or dead, is coincidental.

To my mother, Dorothy Hannon—
with loving memories of a very special bird's nest
that always graces my Christmas tree…
and The Good Life

Special thanks to:

BMC Terrill J. Malvesti, United States Coast Guard
Julie & Karsten Reinemo, Topspin Sportfishing Charters
Erika Mooney, The 'Sconset Trust
Michael Galvin, Nantucket Chamber of Commerce

1

"Sorry to interrupt, sir. But I've got a hot one for you."

Swiveling his desk chair away from the foggy view of Nantucket Harbor, Lieutenant Craig Cole set aside the boat-hours report he'd been reading and gave his executive petty officer his full attention. "What's up?"

"A complaint, sir. From the owner of one of the local charter fishing operations, who isn't happy about a safety citation we issued this afternoon. The captain asked to speak with you, but you were at that special Conservation Commission meeting. I've tried to smooth the waters—pardon the pun—but I'm not making any headway. Now that you're back, it may be best if you take over."

The subtle twitch of his aide's lips was telling. Boatswain's Mate First Class Ben Barlow had been stationed on Nantucket for two years, and he'd been an invaluable—if slightly irreverent—source of information since Craig's arrival four weeks ago, guiding him through several rocky passages. Like the one that appeared to be looming on the horizon.

"What's the story, Barlow?"

The man walked into the office and handed him a copy of the citation. "It's straightforward. Expired flares."

Craig scanned the document. The vessel was an older boat, a thirty-one-foot Wellcraft Suncruiser named the *Lucy Sue*. Although it was equipped with a sufficient number of flares, they were out-of-date. The inspection had been done by the station's newest—and youngest—crew member, but the man seemed to be dependable and conscientious.

"This appears to be in order. What's the problem?"

His aide's lip twitch gave way to a grin. "The captain says we're being hard-nosed. The flares are only a month out-of-date, and she says everyone knows they're good for six months longer than the expiration date—minimum. However, she claims she did intend to replace them before resuming operation this season."

She.

Craig skimmed the name on the citation. Katherine Mac-Donald.

Was the captain's gender the source of Barlow's amusement?

Lowering the sheet of paper, Craig appraised his aide. "I don't care what she says. This is a clear violation of regulations."

"I explained that to her, sir. But she isn't backing down."

Craig's eyes narrowed. "Do you know this woman?"

"No, sir. But I know Chief Medart had great respect for her."

From what he'd heard about his predecessor, Senior Chief Sandra Medart was a solid officer. He'd found no evidence of a lax operation during his brief tenure, though it was more laid-back than he was accustomed to after his past three years at headquarters in Washington, where protocol and procedures reigned supreme.

"Are you suggesting that Chief Medart let personal feelings influence her enforcement of the law, Barlow?"

"No, sir." The man's reply was prompt. "But Captain Mac-Donald has lived on the island her whole life, and she's been doing fishing charters for at least a dozen years. I believe she's descended from an old island whaling family. Her roots here are deep."

"That doesn't exempt her from the law."

"No, sir. She's waiting in my office, sir." The man inclined his head toward the door.

Craig stifled a sigh. Listening to an unjustified tirade hadn't been part of his Friday afternoon agenda on this last day of March, but some backlash was to be expected as Nantucketers got wind of the beefed-up inspection program he'd implemented earlier in the week.

Besides, maintaining positive community relations was part of the job in a command post—especially this one, as he'd been advised when his request for reassignment was granted. An attempt to smooth ruffled feathers without backing down from his firm position on safety-regulation enforcement would be a test of those skills.

"Send her in."

"Yes, sir." His aide retreated as far as the door. "One word of warning, sir. She has red hair—and a temper to go with it." He escaped through the door.

Craig frowned as the petty officer disappeared. The heads-up was appreciated—but how hard could this be? He'd dealt with plenty of distraught people during his career. Handling a small-time charter-fishing boat captain should be a piece of cake—red hair notwithstanding. He'd defuse her anger by remaining calm, cool, and sympathetic...and he'd do his best to keep the encounter as nonconfrontational and pleasant as possible.

But thirty seconds later, when Katherine MacDonald stormed across the office toward his desk, planted her hands on her hips, and pinned him with a glare, his hopes of a cordial discussion disintegrated. Despite her small stature—five-three, five-four at best—she projected a presence as intimidating as any of the hard-as-nails instructors he'd encountered during his Coast

Guard career.

He rose, and her turbulent, flashing green eyes triggered a memory of the worst squall he'd ever encountered. It had happened back in his early days as a rescue swimmer while stationed in Alaska. A small cargo vessel out of Kodiak had lost propulsion and drifted onto the rocks at Cape Trinity, forcing the three crewmen to ditch into the icy, churning sea. As Craig had waited, legs dangling over the edge of the Jayhawk, for the thumbs-up from the flight mechanic to drop into the roiling swells, he'd known in his gut that the dicey, dangerous mission would be forever etched in his memory.

For some disconcerting reason, he felt the same way about this encounter with Katherine MacDonald.

Nevertheless, he did his best to summon up a smile and shift into damage-control mode. "Ms. MacDonald, sorry I wasn't available earlier. Won't you have a seat?" He indicated one of the chairs across from his desk.

"I prefer to stand. This won't take long."

Her curt reply, along with the bristling rage radiating across the expanse of desk between them, left little maneuvering room. So much for leading off with small talk designed to soothe her ire. It was obvious the woman across from him was in no mood for chitchat. There was nothing to do but plunge in and get this over with.

"I understand you have a concern about the safety citation that was issued this afternoon." He kept his tone polite and conversational.

The color rose on her cheeks, drawing his attention to the faint dusting of freckles across the bridge of her nose and the fine lines radiating from the corners of her eyes. The wind and sun could have produced those creases, but the faint smudges of fatigue under the sweep of her lower lashes suggested that out-door living wasn't their only source.

She yanked the crumpled citation out of the pocket of her slicker and tossed it onto his desk, a few tendrils of fiery hair escaping from the clip at her nape to quiver around her face. "This is ridiculous."

Despite his best effort to remain conciliatory, a note of defensiveness crept into Craig's voice. "I disagree. Your flares are expired."

"They last longer than the expiration date. You know that as well as I do. And I was going to replace them before the season opened."

"I'm sorry, Ms. MacDonald. Safety regulations are in place for a reason—and I don't take them lightly."

"Neither do I." Her color deepened as she glowered at him. "Look. You're new here. Fresh out of Washington, from what I hear. This is real life, Lieutenant, where rules aren't quite as cut and dried. I've spent most of my thirty-eight years on this island. I've operated a charter fishing business for fourteen of those years. I don't take chances with the sea, and I would never put anyone who steps onto my boat in danger."

He opened his mouth to respond—but she forged ahead before he could speak.

"Furthermore, I have never been cited for any safety violations, and the *Lucy Sue* has always had a VSC decal from the Coast Guard." She fisted her hands on her hips, her lips tightening. "For your information, I was only taking her for a quick run when that wet-behind-the-ears Coastie pulled alongside for a surprise inspection. Instead of listening to reason, he gave me that." She jabbed the document on Craig's desk. "He even inspected my life jackets—one by one! Under your orders, I presume."

A hot flush rose on Craig's neck at the woman's belligerent attitude and insulting tone. He didn't deserve to be taken to task for doing his job. If previous station commanders had overlooked expired equipment, that was their problem.

"I'm not certain why you're so upset, Ms. MacDonald. All you have to do is buy a few new flares and the problem goes away. They're not expensive."

"It's not the cost. It's the principle. And the problem doesn't go away. A black mark like this on my record will hurt my business. Charter fishing is my livelihood. This is a very competitive market, and potential customers do care about safety ratings." She put her fingertips on his desk and leaned forward, narrowing the gap between their faces to a mere fifteen inches, undaunted by his distinct height advantage as she tipped her chin up to lock gazes with him. "I want mine fixed."

It was hard not to admire her spunk.

"What did you have in mind?"

Her resolute expression hardened. "Here's the deal. I'll get the stupid flares sooner rather than later, even though we both know the ones I have are fine for now. But I want this citation"— she swatted at the crumpled sheet—"wiped off my record."

Expunging a legitimate safety citation wasn't common protocol. And the challenge sparking in the charter captain's irises told him she knew that.

His first inclination was to refuse her request. The rulebook would back him up one hundred percent.

Yet the deep-seated worry…and the echo of profound sadness…in the depths of her eyes held him back.

This was a woman who had endured more than her share of

sorrow. Who'd been knocked down, pushed to the limits, and was fighting to hold on. Who was forging ahead, trying to survive, despite the harsh blows life had dealt.

Kind of like him.

His rigid posture relaxed as he studied her.

Perhaps they had more in common than either of them knew.

As the silence between them lengthened, a flicker of uncertainty displaced Katherine MacDonald's anger. All at once, she backed off several feet and thrust her hands into the pockets of her slicker.

Interesting.

This feisty woman didn't mind in-your-face confrontations to protect her business. But let someone probe too deep, delve beneath her bluster, and her protection strategy was to back off—fast.

Tipping up her chin, she made a valiant attempt to recapture her earlier bravado. But her challenge came off more distraught than defiant. "Well? Do we have a deal?"

"Let me think about it."

She mashed her lips together. "Fine." Though her tone said otherwise. "Your people know where to find me. In the meantime, I'll get the flares." She turned on her heel and strode out the door.

For a full minute, Craig remained standing behind his desk, nerve endings tingling. Pulse pounding. Lungs pumping. The same physical reaction he always had after a perilous rescue mission.

What was going on?

And why did he feel so rattled....off balance...irritated?

Whatever the cause of his unsettling mental state, he needed to get a handle on his reaction. There was no place for emotion in the Coast Guard. Succumbing to even a few seconds of debilitating fear as a rescue swimmer could have meant the difference between life and death for himself or the victims he'd been sent to save.

Nor could he let emotion play a role here, as controller of a search and rescue command center, where deployment decisions should be governed by the pure facts and figures of the Mayday.

As for emotion in his personal life—he'd kept a firm rein on that too these past three years… leaving his off-duty life as dull and mind-numbing as the hours he'd spent shuffling papers behind a desk in Washington. But at least it had been livable.

Katherine MacDonald, however, had managed to prod a few buried emotions awake. No surprise, since emotion could be her middle name. And hers hadn't just run high, they'd exploded. Even now, in her absence, the room continued to vibrate with them. Not much likelihood the word *dull* was in her vocabulary— or in anyone's who came into contact with her.

A discreet knock sounded on the door, and Barlow stepped inside, his grin still in place. "Checking on survivors, sir."

Ignoring his aide's comment, Craig picked up the pristine copy of the safety citation he'd skimmed earlier and handed it over, leaving the crumpled version untouched on his desk. "See that this is held for a couple of days before we file it."

"Yes, sir." Amusement glinted in his eyes.

Fixing the executive petty officer with a steely look, Craig folded his arms across his chest. "Is there a problem?"

To Barlow's credit, his demeanor grew more serious. Smart man. Not only did he balance his slight impertinence with a likable manner and razor-sharp skills, he knew where to draw the line.

"No, sir."

As his aide beat a hasty retreat, Craig walked to the window and surveyed the harbor. It was far emptier than it would be in a couple of months, but a fair number of boats occupied slips— including Katherine MacDonald's.

Strange.

Half an hour ago, he hadn't known the woman existed. Yet in the course of one brief conversation, she'd managed to rouse a boatload of emotions in him—most of which were best left undisturbed.

As for his plans for a low-key, relaxing weekend?

They, too, had been disrupted.

Also thanks to one certain red-haired fishing boat captain.

* * *

"Mommy, Mommy, Mrs. Shaw and me baked cookies! Chocolate chip!"

As Kate bent to hug her daughter, she glanced over the four-year-old's shoulder toward Edith Shaw, standing a few feet away. "I bet that was fun, honey. It sounds like you had a happy day."

Her stocky, gray-haired Lighthouse Lane neighbor gave a reassuring nod. "Maddie and I had a fine afternoon."

Some of the tension in Kate's shoulders eased. But it would take a lot longer for the rest of it to dissipate after her unpleasant encounter less than an hour ago with the new Coast Guard commander.

"You seem stressed, my dear." The older woman gave Kate a discerning perusal. "Why don't you have a cup of tea before you head home?"

"I should go next door to The Devon Rose if I want tea instead of taking advantage of your hospitality."

"That would be more elegant, no question about it. Heather serves a wonderful proper British afternoon tea." Then Edith winked. "But I guarantee she won't offer you home-baked chocolate chip cookies. As for taking advantage of me...that's nonsense. We're neighbors, for goodness' sake. You've listened to me gripe on numerous occasions. I'm happy to return the favor."

"Is it that obvious I need to vent?"

"In a word...yes. The steam coming from your ears was my first clue. Problems with the *Lucy Sue?*"

"Minor compared to my problems with Lieutenant Craig Cole."

"You've met the invisible man?" The woman's eyebrows peaked.

"Who's the invisible man?"

Whoops.

Maddie's question underscored the need for prudence when discussing grown-up topics in her presence.

"It's kind of a joke, honey." Kate swept a few strands of hair off her daughter's forehead. "No one has seen much of the new commander at the Coast Guard station, so people call him the invisible man."

"Maybe he's busy."

"I expect that's true." Harassing law-abiding citizens was surely a time suck.

"Maddie, why don't you finish building your castle in the sunroom while your mommy and I have tea?" Edith leaned down to the youngster. "After we're done, you can tell us a story about the people who live there."

"Okay."

As Maddie skipped off, Kate shook her head. "Talk about little pitchers."

"She doesn't miss much, that's for sure."

"No more problems today?"

"Not a one. She's fine, Kate. Come on, let's have that tea."

"Could we make it coffee instead?"

"Heather still hasn't converted you, I see."

"It's a lost cause."

"She's made inroads with me—but I still like my coffee too. You're on." Edith led the way toward her Early American-style kitchen, pulling two mugs from pegs on the wall.

"Where's Chester?" Kate took a seat at the familiar hickory table that had hosted more than its share of gab sessions with her neighbor and propped her chin in her palm.

"In the garden, finishing up the renovations on the guest cottage." She shook her head as she bustled about the homey room. "I'm not convinced it will be ready to rent out this season, though. My good husband has been futzing around with it for months, and the tourists will be descending before we know it."

"And life will get even busier." Kate sighed and selected a cookie from the plate on the table.

After pulling a pitcher of cream from the refrigerator, Edith studied her. "Do I detect a hint of pessimism in that comment?"

"Maybe."

"That's not like you. You've always kept a positive attitude despite problems that would have made most people cave long ago."

"You and Chester can claim the lion's share of credit for that. If you hadn't agreed to watch Maddie while I work, and if Chester hadn't stepped in as my first mate, I doubt I'd have made it."

"Yes, you would. You're a survivor, Kate MacDonald. But even the best of us can get discouraged on a bad day. And yours sounds like a doozy." She dropped her volume. "Starting with

Maddie's asthma attack at four in the morning."

"It wasn't a great beginning." Kate angled her head toward the window-rimmed room Chester had added to the back of the kitchen. Maddie was busy with her blocks and oblivious to the adult conversation, the panic-filled attack in the wee hours of the morning, the tears, the nebulizer treatment already a distant memory.

Too bad the same wasn't true for her. But after each episode, the agony of watching her daughter struggle for air and the desperate helplessness that twisted her stomach into knots stayed with her. Sometimes a hefty dose of guilt was thrown in for good measure too. Like now.

Setting aside the uneaten cookie, Kate massaged her forehead with her fingertips. "The thing is, I know the triggers for her attacks. I should have taken her ski mask yesterday when we went grocery shopping. She breathed in too much cold air."

"Don't beat yourself up, Kate. It was a beautiful day until that front decided to drop in unannounced."

"Nantucket weather is unpredictable. I should have been prepared."

Edith filled both mugs from the coffeemaker on the counter and took a seat at the table. "Only one person who walked on this earth was perfect, Kate. And he doesn't expect anyone to repeat that feat. He just expects us to try our best. And you always do that. This morning's asthma episode is history. Let's move on to what happened today."

Thank heaven for Edith's practical, no-nonsense approach that always helped her regain perspective on nerve-racking days like this.

She took a fortifying sip of the hot brew and told her neighbor about the citation.

"That's a technicality." Edith waved a hand in dismissal. "You replace the flares every year. Besides, they last longer than that."

"That's what I told the by-the-book lieutenant, who instituted the beefed-up inspection program. I paid him a visit to express my…displeasure."

Edith quirked an eyebrow. "How did that go?"

As the scene replayed in her mind, Kate frowned and ran a finger around the rim of her mug. Warmth seeped into the tip— and up the back of her neck. "Not very well. I suppose I may have been a bit…vocal…in my opinions."

Edith didn't attempt to hide her amusement as she took a sip of coffee. "I wish I'd been a fly on the wall. How did he react?"

The heat on Kate's neck rose to her cheeks. Why, oh why, had she been born a redhead?

"Not well. In the end, I agreed to replace them right away if he erased the citation from my record. He said he'd think about it."

"Interesting." Edith stirred her coffee. "What do you think convinced your by-the-book commander to consider overlooking the violation?"

Nothing she'd said, that was for sure. Whatever diplomacy skills she possessed had deserted her during their meeting. By the time she'd faced off with him across the desk and delivered her ultimatum, she'd braced for a refusal based on her attitude alone.

But his cobalt eyes had softened a fraction—meaning he'd seen far more than she'd wanted to reveal. Breached the defenses around her heart. That had been seriously uncomfortable.

Still, if whatever he'd detected had convinced him to cut her some slack, why complain? She'd accomplished her mission.

And it wasn't as if their paths were likely to cross very often once this was resolved.

"Kate?"

At Edith's prompt, she refocused. "I don't know why he eased off. I guess he had second thoughts."

"I suppose that's possible." Although a note of skepticism in her tone said otherwise. "So what does the invisible man look like?"

"I didn't pay that much attention to his appearance."

"Oh, come now. You must have noticed the basics. Height, hair color, age."

Yeah, she had. It was hard not to notice a man who was lean and toned, with broad shoulders and a powerful chest to go with the take-charge manner and commanding bearing that radiated strength and competence.

Details Edith did *not* need to know. The basics would suffice.

"Six-one or -two, I'd guess. Dark blond hair. Fortyish."

"Attractive?"

She shrugged and tried for nonchalance. "I suppose some women would think so."

"Are you one of them?"

Oh, for pity's sake. They were back on the subject of romance again—a topic her neighbor had been broaching with increasing frequency over the past few months.

"He's not my type, Edith—and I'm not in the market anyway." She swallowed, dropping her gaze to the black depths of her coffee. "There was only one man for me."

The woman reached out and covered Kate's hand with her own, all traces of humor vanishing. "Mac was one of a kind, Kate. No question about that. But he wouldn't want you to live the rest of your life alone if another man came along who was worthy of your love."

"No one could ever take his place. Besides, my life is crazy enough without adding romance to the mix." Motioning toward the sunroom, she rose. "Let's go see Maddie's castle." Without waiting for a response, she picked up her mug and walked away from the table.

But a few minutes later, as she and Edith listened to the youngster's imaginative story about the castle she'd constructed from her blocks, the most annoying thing happened.

Every time Maddie mentioned Prince Charming, an image of Lieutenant Craig Cole came to mind.

2

Skin tingling from the salt spray, Kate filled her lungs with the bracing air as the *Lucy Sue*'s bow cut a wide swath through the choppy seas off Great Point. Nantucket might be living up to her nickname as The Gray Lady on this Sunday morning, but as far as Kate was concerned, this wild, windswept, isolated speck of land twenty-six miles from the mainland was beautiful no matter her wardrobe.

She tuned in to the engine, listening for any hint of the slight rattle that had plagued the *Lucy Sue* for the past week. Nada. Thank heaven for neighbors like Chester, whose magic touch with all things mechanical kept the boat's sometimes-temperamental engine purring. With the season about ready to kick off, downtime would be disastrous. The twice daily trips with a boatful of amateur anglers paid the bills.

Flexing her knees to absorb the chop, Kate angled toward the majestic whitewashed lighthouse that dominated the long expanse of pristine beach populated only by a few gulls on this dreary morning. Not unusual. Few visitors ventured to the remotest of the island's three lighthouses even in the best of weather, and hardy locals rarely made the trek on a day like this.

Except for Mac. He'd loved this spot, rain or shine.

Pressure built in her throat, and Kate checked her watch. Time to head back and pick up Maddie. It would be wrong to take advantage of Edith's generosity—and thinking about the man who'd filled her days with sunshine…and whose loss had left an aching void in her heart…would only dampen her spirits.

She swung the wheel to port and pointed the *Lucy Sue* back toward the harbor, scanning the undulating sea. In two months, this prime fishing ground would be dotted with crafts of all sizes, but today she had the open expanse to herself.

Or…did she?

What was that bobbing orange speck in the distance?

Easing back on the throttle, she squinted through the mist. It could be debris. But after pulling more than her share of too-confident swimmers out of these waters, she'd learned an important lesson.

Never overestimate people's common sense.

Without taking her gaze off the spot where the orange speck kept disappearing among the swells, she felt for the binoculars secured within reaching distance of the helm. Fitting them to her eyes, she planted her feet in a wide, steadying stance and focused on the object.

In general, the seven-by-thirty magnification was sufficient. But today it couldn't overcome the obscuring combination of distance, mist, and the rocking motion of the boat. All she could tell with any certainty was that the object was about fifty yards offshore and moving on a steady, purposeful course parallel to the beach.

Meaning it was alive.

And it wasn't a seal or a fish. Fluorescent orange wasn't in the marine life palette of Nantucket.

That left only one possibility.

It was human.

Irene Hannon

Lowering the binoculars, Kate huffed out a breath. What kind of idiot would go for a dip off Great Point? These were dangerous swimming waters any season of the year, let alone in early April, when the threat of hypothermia amplified the peril.

It was obvious the swimmer churning through the swells didn't understand the risks—or didn't consider them to be a problem. Hard to decide which was worse. The former smacked of stupidity, the latter of arrogance.

In either case, someone needed to pound some sense into the guy's head. And it *was* a guy—even if that conclusion reeked of stereotypical sexism.

Compressing her lips, Kate swung the *Lucy Sue* hard to starboard, shifted into full throttle, and barreled straight toward the bobbing orange speck.

Whoever she found cavorting in the heaving gray swells was about to get an earful.

* * *

One, two, three, four, five, breathe. One, two, three, four, five, breathe. One, two, three, four, five, breathe.
Encased in his neoprene wetsuit, Craig cut through the swells with powerful, even strokes, propelling himself forward with strong, steady kicks of his flippers despite the forty-two-degree water. After all the missions he'd swum in the Arctic, this was a bathtub. The chop was distracting, and the riptide had been a tad annoying, but neither had disrupted his bilateral breathing rhythm. After fifteen minutes of steady swimming, he wasn't even winded.

Because he was in his element.

It may have taken him three years of mind-numbing boredom sitting behind a desk in Washington to come to terms with his sorrow and anger, but returning to field duty had been a sound decision—for a host of reasons.

An icy wave smacked him in the face, and Craig sucked in a mouthful of water. Coughed. Lost his rhythm.

Blast.

He'd let the sea surprise him, score a point. Bad mistake. One he'd vowed never to let happen again. His last mistake had cost him too—

"Hey! Hey, you!"

At the shouted summons, Craig broke his rhythm again—this time on purpose. Riding the swells, he lifted his head and searched for the source.

The name of the boat rocking on the waves a few yards away clicked into focus first.

Lucy Sue.

Meaning the human hurricane couldn't be far behind.

Taking a deep breath, Craig tipped up his chin.

Sure enough, the voice belonged to none other than Katherine MacDonald. And she was in a snit once again, judging by her ruddy color and tense posture as she glared down at him, her wind-tossed red hair whipping about her face.

The full blast of her fury was coming. The signs were all there. He should prep for battle.

Instead, the image of an artist's rendering he'd once seen of Grace O'Malley materialized in his mind. With her proud bearing and glorious hair, Katherine MacDonald could be that legendary Irish pirate queen. And the daggers shooting from her eyes were—

"…recreational swimming area!"

As the tail end of her comment registered, he refocused. "What?"

Her cheeks got pinker. "I said, are you crazy? This is not a recreational swimming area!" She had to yell to be heard above the hum of the engine and the waves slapping against the side of the boat.

"I'm fine."

"You can't be fine! The water's freezing! And there's a bad riptide here. Get to shore!" She flapped her hand toward the beach, as if shooing a recalcitrant puppy back from the edge of a busy street.

She didn't recognize him.

But why should she? His wetsuit, swim cap, and goggles left few identifying features exposed.

Bobbing on the swells, he considered his options.

The path of least resistance would be to remain anonymous, acquiesce, and retreat to the beach. He'd been about ready to head toward shore anyway. Why fuel her ire?

Instead, he lifted his goggles and settled them on top of the orange swim cap. "I can handle this sea, Ms. MacDonald."

Her dumbstruck reaction as his identity registered was ample reward for his riskier choice.

Unfortunately, her muteness was short-lived.

"I don't believe this! You, of all people, should know better than to swim in seas like this! Alone, no less! And you cited *me* for a safety violation?"

Great comeback. The lady was fast on the uptake.

"I'm trained to swim in worse conditions than these. And I'm well-equipped."

She dismissed his explanation with a flip of her hand. "That may be true, but no one in his right mind would put himself into dangerous conditions without cause. Do you have a death wish or something?"

He frowned.

Of course she was exaggerating…but all at once his interest in prolonging their verbal sparring match evaporated.

Pulling his goggles back down, he prepared to resume his swim.

The red-haired spitfire must have sensed his intent because she called out again. "I can't in good conscience leave anyone alone in these waters, especially in this weather."

He studied her over his shoulder as he treaded water, buoyant on the rising swells. She was still standing by the side of the boat, gripping the rail, watching him.

Ignoring her comment, he resumed his course, swimming parallel to the shore.

Thirty seconds later, the hum of her boat sounded behind him.

Craig kept swimming for two more minutes, the boat pacing him. She wasn't backing down—surprise, surprise.

Since he'd stayed out as long as he'd planned and the cold seeping through his neoprene insulation was beginning to get uncomfortable, may as well call it a day.

Altering his course, he aimed for shore. Let Katherine Mac-Donald assume she'd won this battle. Why make waves when he was finished anyway?

Had she caught him at the beginning of his swim, however, he'd have put up with the audience—and she'd have discovered he could be as strong-willed as she was.

That revelation wasn't going to happen today.

But if he was a betting man, he'd lay odds it was coming.

* * *

The lieutenant had relented.

Huh.

Not what she'd expected from a rule-bound man who didn't seem prone to capitulation. A battle of wills had appeared to be imminent.

Kate planted her fists on her hips and watched as he surged through the swells with powerful strokes, doing her best to stifle the flicker of admiration fanned to life by his masterful physical control and his command of the water.

But even proficient swimmers shouldn't venture into hazardous seas alone. It was folly to feel invincible around the ocean, no matter how strong or well-equipped you were. And a Coast Guard lieutenant should know that.

The instant he emerged from the water, Kate swung the *Lucy Sue* to port and picked up speed, focusing on more pleasant thoughts as the boat plowed through the waves. Like the pizza dinner she and Maddie had planned for tonight, followed by a movie of her daughter's choice. No doubt her current favorite, *The Lion King*. This would be their fourth viewing—but who cared? Cuddling with her daughter under an afghan, a cozy fire burning in the grate, was a perfect way to spend a chilly evening.

Well...almost perfect.

A spray of water misted her face, leaving the taste of salt behind.

Perfect would be having Mac with them. The man who'd

stolen her heart had had a remarkable gift for turning ordinary days into special occasions, his infectious *joie de vivre* and go-with-the-flow attitude carrying everyone along with him.

Had he been here, tonight would be different. Less planned, more spontaneous. Instead of pizza, he might suggest chocolate chip waffles. Rather than sitting on the couch, he'd drag out their folding chairs, make popcorn, and have them pretend they were at the old hall in 'Sconset that showed family movies in the summer. Given his penchant for classic musicals, he'd resurrect their vintage copy of *The Sound of Music* and encourage them all to sing along, his off-key baritone and contagious laugh ringing through the house.

Mac had embraced life—and he'd never sweated the small stuff.

A lesson the stiff, stuffy lieutenant she'd left on Great Point would do well to learn.

Kate tightened her grip on the helm and glowered that direction. The island's new Coast Guard commander seemed focused *only* on the small stuff. Case in point? The nonsensical citation she'd been issued.

But that little tirade of yours at Great Point didn't help your situation, you know.

Her scowl deepened as she neared the harbor entrance and passed diminutive Brant Point Lighthouse adjacent to the Coast Guard station.

Yeah, yeah, she knew.

Instead of reading him the riot act and following him like a persistent seagull follows a boat, she could have accepted his explanation and pointed the *Lucy Sue* toward home.

Yet how could she have left anyone—even the disagreeable

lieutenant—alone in the waters off Great Point?

The wharf came into sight, and Kate cut back the throttle.

Simple answer? She couldn't. She'd dug in her heels for his own good, whether he appreciated it or not.

Not being the obvious conclusion.

And that didn't bode well for a favorable response to her request—okay, fine...demand—that he wipe the citation off her record.

An outcome that seemed increasingly remote in light of their back-to-back unpleasant encounters.

3

"I have to run a couple of errands, Barlow." Craig stopped in the doorway of his aide's office. "I'll be back in an hour."

Ben offered him a jaunty salute. "No problem. I've got it covered."

"There's not much to cover. It's been a quiet Monday."

"Enjoy it while it lasts. Once the day-trippers and summer people arrive, you won't have a minute to call your own. And some of the calls we get are a stitch. Last year, the guy who forgot to install his drain plug and ended up sinking his boat won the prize."

"I can't wait."

"Trust me. You can."

A smile tugging at his lips, Craig took advantage of the springlike weather and struck off down Easton Street on foot. A walk around town was overdue. From what he'd gleaned about his predecessor, most Nantucketers had known her on sight, and both locals and crew had liked and respected her. According to Barlow, she'd excelled at the PR aspect of the job.

It was time to show his face in the community.

He turned onto South Beach Street, and in mere minutes he reached the heart of the historic town, with its cobblestone streets and labyrinth of tiny lanes. His dark blue slacks and the matching shirt with twin silver bars on the collar that signaled his rank identified him at a glance as the new commander, and as he strolled around he drew more than a few curious perusals. Only year-rounders populated the quiet town center on this early April Monday, and when he nodded and smiled in response to their discreet perusal, several approached to welcome him.

Forty-five minutes later, after picking up a paper at The Hub and stopping at a few other spots Barlow had identified as local hangouts, he ambled down Main Street toward the harbor. In three short blocks, the cobblestones of the town's primary thoroughfare merged with Straight Wharf, where many of the commercial boats were docked.

The *Lucy Sue* among them.

At the entrance to the wharf, Craig hesitated. The original copy of Katherine MacDonald's citation was in his pocket—but this matter didn't require his personal attention. One of his crew members could handle the resolution of such a minor violation.

Except it wasn't minor to Ms. MacDonald, as she'd made very clear. And as long as he was in the area, it wouldn't hurt to stop by and see if he could smooth out the turbulent waters between them—all in the interest of creating positive PR, of course. Why else would he put himself in the path of the human hurricane again?

A few other possibilities popped to mind. Like appealing green eyes that flashed with life and passion…and the intriguing juxtaposition of her delicate physical appearance with a strong character. . . and vibrant hair that sparked with every movement.

But only a masochist would want to deal with her temper.

He was here on business. Period. And once it was done, he wasn't going to linger.

Picking up his pace, Craig strode past the shuttered souvenir shops. Within minutes he found the *Lucy Sue,* gently rocking in her slip on the wharf. There was no sign of the red-haired skipper—or anyone else. No surprise there, considering most owners wintered their boats on the mainland. Those who didn't spent but a handful of hours aboard in the off-season.

So what was with the flutter of disappointment in the pit of his stomach? He should be happy to avoid another exchange with the argumentative captain.

But he wasn't.

Rather than try to analyze his odd reaction, he propped his fists on his hips and surveyed the boat at close range. The citation had indicated that the *Lucy Sue* was an older model, and she was. The boat had to have been built twenty, twenty-five years ago. Yet she was well maintained. There was no evidence of barnacles below the waterline, nor any indication of oxidation topside—suggesting the fiberglass hull was polished and waxed on a regular basis. The deck was stain-free, and the teak trim had been varnished rather than allowed to weather to whitish-gray. The finish appeared to be fresh too, free of obvious chips or scuffs.

Anyone who went to such effort to keep a boat shipshape was likely to be as diligent about mechanical maintenance—and safety. And in light of the number of charter slips, Ms. MacDonald hadn't been exaggerating about the competition.

No wonder the flare citation had upset her.

And given the traces of worry and sorrow he'd glimpsed as she'd squared off with him across his desk on Friday, the last thing she needed in her life was more stress.

So if she'd followed through and replaced the flares, as she'd promised, disposing of the citation in his pocket was going to be his top priority this afternoon.

* * *

What was the Coast Guard commander doing at the *Lucy Sue?*

Kate's step faltered as she turned a corner on Straight Wharf and caught sight of the tall officer standing beside her boat. Another skirmish with the line-toeing lieutenant was *not* in her plans for the day.

His back was to her, giving her an excellent view of his broad shoulders as he scrutinized the *Lucy Sue.* Should she beat a hasty retreat before he noticed her?

No.

Running from problems didn't solve them.

If he'd decided to let the citation stand, she may as well get the bad news now rather than later. And his presence suggested the news was bad rather than good. Why else would he come in person, except to turn the tables and wield his authority by scuttling her request? After the way she'd treated him in their previous encounters, he could very well take advantage of the opportunity to put her in her place.

Shoulders slumping, she shifted the bag she was toting from one arm to the other. Then she forced her feet to carry her forward, her sport shoes noiseless on the wharf.

A few feet away from the grim reaper she drew a fortifying breath. "Planning to do another inspection, Lieutenant?" She tried to keep her tone neutral, but a touch of defiance crept in.

He swung toward her, his features etched with surprise—and another emotion she couldn't identify.

"That wasn't in my plans."

"Following up on the one already done, then."

"Yes. I was in town anyway and thought I'd drop by."

"I got the flares." She edged past him on the finger pier, juggling the bag as she prepared to board.

"Let me hold that for you." He took the sack from her before she could protest, glancing at the package of spark plugs on top. "Engine problems?"

Rather than give him a direct answer, she swung into the boat and reached for the bag. "I'm always prepared."

"You do your own maintenance?"

"Most of it. My neighbor helps me with the trickier issues. And speaking of being prepared, let me show you the new flares." She ducked into the cabin, retrieved the flares, and rejoined him thirty seconds later on the wharf. "As you'll see, I'm covered for the new season."

The lieutenant took the flares in silence, scanned the expiration dates, and handed them back. "Everything appears to be in order."

"So what happens next?" She braced for bad news.

He reached into the pocket of his slacks and withdrew the original citation, which had been folded into neat, precise squares. Tore it into small pieces. Disposed of them in a trash can a few steps away.

She stared at him. "Does that mean...are you going to expunge it from my record?"

"Yes."

"Why?"

"Your request was reasonable—even if you weren't." A touch of amusement sparked in his irises. "Do you always overreact when you're angry?"

She stiffened. "I've been told I don't suffer fools gladly."

He cocked one eyebrow but remained silent.

Oh, for pity's sake, Kate! The man has just done you a huge favor, and you insult him instead of thanking him? How ungracious is that?

Cheeks flaming, she shoved her hands into the front pockets

of her jeans and prepared to eat crow. "Look, can we start over?"

"I'm game."

"Thanks." She moistened her lips. "The thing is, I appreciate your consideration. I'm sure you noticed the *Lucy Sue* is an older model. It's not as jazzy as most of the other charter boats, nor does it have all the bells and whistles. A clean safety record is a selling point I can use in my advertising to help me compete. Without it…" She shrugged.

"Understood." He folded his arms. "My executive petty officer tells me you've been at this awhile, Ms. MacDonald."

The wind whipped a lock of hair across her cheek, and she tucked it behind her ear. "Yes. My father-in-law started the business. He retired and passed it on to me and my husband when we married. But I've been fishing my whole life." May as well go the whole nine yards with the olive branch. "By the way, my friends call me Kate."

"As in *Kiss Me, Kate?* Based on *Taming of the Shrew?*"

She grimaced. "I suppose that's a fair question in light of our encounters. And I apologize for my bad temper. You hit me on a rough couple of days. Believe it or not, Lieutenant, despite my red hair I usually stay on a pretty even keel."

"The name is Craig. And I suppose I'll find out the truth of that for myself if our paths cross again."

"I expect they will on occasion. It's not a big island."

"Well—paperwork awaits."

"Thank you again for tearing up the citation."

"Not a problem. Take care." After giving her a mock salute, he headed toward Main Street.

She waited until he disappeared, then boarded the *Lucy Sue* to tackle her chores…and rethink her opinion of the new Coast

Guard commander. It was possible her initial assessment of him as a stuffy, rigid, rule follower had been a tad too hasty—and a boatload too harsh.

Still, one cordial exchange wasn't sufficient proof she'd been wrong about his character. She'd have to see a lot more of him before she could be certain his judgment was sounder than she'd first thought.

And despite their rocky start and her earlier resolve to avoid him as much as possible, that prospect held far more appeal than it should.

* * *

"I smell cinnamon! Oh, goodie!" Maddie broke free of Kate's grasp and barreled straight for the plate of cinnamon toast waiting on the hickory table in Edith's cozy kitchen.

"I gave her breakfast already, Edith. You didn't have to do that." Kate entered her neighbor's back door at a more sedate pace, stopping two steps into the room.

"I wanted to. I like doing things for people I care about. Have some coffee."

"I can't. I'm already running late."

"You can be at the high school in five minutes. I'll pour you a cup to go." Edith retrieved an insulated mug with a lid from the cabinet and lifted the pot from the coffeemaker. "Besides, I wanted to tell you about an interesting experience I had last night."

The woman's studied casualness put Kate on alert. "What happened?"

"I met your lieutenant at the market." She added cream to the coffee with a quick tip of the pitcher. "I must admit, his manner wasn't at all what I anticipated from your description. He was charming."

Kate's cheeks warmed. "I've amended my opinion a bit."

"Since when?"

"Since he erased the citation from my record yesterday."

"Did he, now?" The older woman secured the lid on the mug and passed it over. "Must have been your charm."

Kate made a face at her. "Very funny." She hoisted her purse higher on her shoulder and changed the subject. "I've got to run. It sets a bad example when the teachers are tardy. Call me if you have any problems with Maddie."

"I've got the nebulizer routine down if we need it. Don't worry."

"It's hard not to."

"You know what Mac would have said."

"Yes." The corners of her mouth rose a hair. "'Don't look for trouble.'" She leaned over and hugged the gray-haired woman, who was more like family than a mere neighbor or friend. "I'm sorry I've had to call on you so often this school year. I can't remember ever being asked to sub this much. But the extra money's been a godsend."

Edith waved the apology aside. "I don't mind in the least. Maddie's a charmer. And speaking of charmers—the lieutenant fits that definition in my book."

Once Edith sank her teeth into a topic, she was as hard to shake loose as the island's notorious deer ticks. "Like I said, he's not as bad as I first thought." She reached for the doorknob.

"He doesn't think you're too bad, either, despite your show of temper."

Kate swung back. "He talked about me?"

"Only after I happened to mention we were neighbors."

Ha. There was no *happen to* about it. When the Lighthouse Lane matron was on a mission, she could be as single-minded as a Nantucket whaler of old in hot pursuit of his quarry.

Kate clutched her purse strap as her pulse accelerated. "You didn't tell him what I said about him, did you?"

"Of course not." Edith gave an indignant sniff. "That was between the two of us. I merely mentioned I'd known you for years and that you were a wonderful person—and a hard worker. He said he'd been impressed by your determination and complimented the *Lucy Sue.* Called her a fine boat, and said you'd taken great care of her."

"What else did you two talk about?"

"Nothing." The corners of Edith's mouth turned down in disgust. "His cell phone rang just as the conversation was getting interesting. Some emergency at the station."

Thank heaven!

"I have to run. I'll be back around three-thirty."

"Bye, Mommy." Maddie waved and took another huge bite of cinnamon toast.

Kate walked over to her daughter and gave her a quick peck on the cheek. "Be good for Mrs. Shaw."

"I will."

"See you later, Edith." With a wave, Kate let herself out.

As she navigated the maze of narrow streets that led to the school, she tried to focus on her lesson plan for the day.

No go.

All she could think about was a broad-shouldered lieutenant who, according to Edith, admired her determination.

She winced as she sidestepped a pothole.

That was a kind way to describe her approach in their first two altercations. Hostility and rudeness would be more accurate.

It appeared the man was not only generous about forgiving transgressions but accomplished in the art of diplomacy.

At least he didn't seem to be holding her temper against her.

But while determination was a fine attribute, it was too bad he hadn't found a few other less—strident—qualities to admire about her.

Shaking her head, Kate crossed the street. What a silly waste of brain power. The lieutenant had wiped her record clean. That was what mattered. She shouldn't care what he thought about her.

Yet, much to her annoyance, she did.

4

"**M**y stars, look who's here!"

At Edith's whispered comment, Kate followed her line of sight as they walked down the church aisle on Sunday.

Seated in a pew halfway down on the left was none other than Lieutenant Craig Cole. Only his back was visible, but there was no mistaking that dark blond hair.

Snagging her neighbor's arm, Kate indicated a pew beside her. "This is fine."

The older woman kept moving, dragging Kate along with her. "We never sit this far back."

"Edith." Kate hissed her name, and the older woman paused. "Maddie and I are going to sit here today."

After a brief hesitation, Edith shrugged. "Suit yourself. We'll see you after the service." She tucked her arm through Chester's and made a beeline for the pew behind the commander.

"Mommy, how come we aren't sitting with Mr. and Mrs. Shaw?" Maddie's childish soprano carried throughout the house of worship.

Dipping her head, Kate ushered her daughter into the pew. "I thought it would be fun to sit somewhere different today." She pitched her voice extra low. *Please let Maddie take the hint!*

No such luck. Her daughter's version of whispering was to lean close while speaking in a normal tone. "But I can't see the front. We're too far back."

Bribery was *not* the best way to control a child's behavior—but there were rare exceptions.

Today qualified.

"Maddie, honey, it's just for this one week. And if you stay very quiet, I'll take you to Downyflake afterward."

The promise of a visit to the well-loved doughnut establishment did the trick. There wasn't a peep out of Maddie for the rest of the service. She folded her hands in her lap, sang along with the hymns she knew, and kept her attention fixed on the sanctuary. She was the picture of piousness.

In contrast, Kate fidgeted throughout the entire service. She crossed and uncrossed her legs, trying to find a comfortable position. She wandered off the melody of a familiar hymn, arching the eyebrows of a few nearby congregants. She couldn't concentrate on Reverend Kaizer's sermon.

All because of the Coast Guard commander sitting a dozen rows away.

It was ridiculous.

But there wasn't a thing she could do about it.

In the end, she stopped trying to ignore him and allowed herself a few discreet peeks his direction. Dressed in civilian clothes, he projected a far different aura than when in uniform. Less authoritarian. Less severe. More human—and approachable. He also had excellent taste. His dark gray slacks, white shirt, and charcoal tweed jacket conveyed a quiet, casual elegance that suited his lean, muscular frame.

As the organ struck up the final hymn, Kate helped Maddie put on her coat. How providential that they'd driven themselves to church instead of hitching a ride with Edith and Chester, as usual. Having their own wheels would allow them to escape fast.

The instant the last note of the hymn died away, she hustled Maddie out the door and toward the car, exchanging greetings with members of the congregation without slowing her pace. Only after they pulled out of their parking place and were almost at their destination in the south end of town did her respiration return to normal.

They were safe.

Safe.

Frowning, Kate swung into the last parking space in Downyflake's lot. And her brow remained furrowed as she and Maddie joined the long line that spilled out the front door.

Why didn't she feel safe around the new commander? And why had she felt the need to escape from him?

It had nothing to do with his position of authority. Yes, the citation had been upsetting…but she'd felt angry, not threatened. Nor had she felt in the least intimidated—or unsafe—when she'd marched over to his office and laid into him about it, nor when she'd rebuked him for risking his neck off Great Point. The unsafe feeling was more…personal…than that.

And it had started that moment in his office when he'd somehow tapped into her private sorrows and deepest insecurities. He couldn't know what they were—but he knew they were there…and his ability to breach her defenses, see more than she was comfortable sharing, was unsettling.

That wasn't what made her feel vulnerable, either, however.

So what was the cause of this strange unease?

Come on, Kate. You know the answer to that question.

Her breath hitched as the line moved forward.

Yeah, she did.

The truth was, for the first time since she'd lost Mac, she'd noticed a man. That little flutter in her stomach was pure, unadulterated attraction.

"Mommy, you're hurting my hand!"

At Maddie's protest, Kate loosened her grip and bent to give the youngster a hug. "I'm sorry, honey. We're almost to the counter." Her breathing grew choppy as she struggled to rein in her galloping pulse. "What kind of doughnut are you going to get?"

"Sugar."

"How come I knew that?" It took every ounce of her willpower to adopt a teasing tone—and to engage the left side of her brain so she could analyze the situation logically as she urged Maddie forward in the line.

Fact one—no matter what Edith thought, she wasn't ready for another romance.

Fact two—the lieutenant wasn't her type. He was nothing like Mac. With his agreeable, relaxed attitude and easygoing charm, her husband had viewed life through a lens that captured nuances of color and texture rather than mere black and white.

Fact three—while the odd magnetic pull she felt toward the new Coast Guard commander was real, it had to be an anomaly. Perhaps induced by the power of Edith's suggestion. Or perhaps she was drawn to him because he'd caught her during a vulnerable stretch, with her shaky finances and concerns about Maddie adding to her stress. Anyone in her situation would be attracted to someone who radiated competence and whose shoulders seemed capable of carrying the heaviest load.

His empathetic blue eyes had nothing at all to do with her reaction.

She mashed her lips together and lifted her chin.

That was her story—and she was sticking to it.

* * *

As Craig slid behind the wheel of his late-model Camry, he surveyed the modest church. A few people remained near the front door, but most had departed after exchanging a few words with him. It had been a worthwhile morning, both from a spiritual and PR perspective. He'd also met quite a few of the locals.

Edith Shaw had been there too. According to Kate's neighbor, who'd managed to ferret quite a bit of information out of him during their short walk to the back of church after the service, the charter captain had also attended. But she was nowhere to be seen when they emerged onto the small lawn.

Probably just as well. She'd been intruding on his thoughts too often as it was. But why had she run off so fast?

Craig guided his car through the town's narrow streets, toward the small bakery/restaurant across from the market. As Barlow had promised, the food was tasty—and the tab was affordable. An exception on an island where most prices were elevated from the mainland. The high cost of living on Nantucket had been a shocker.

As he approached his destination, the packed lot and the throng at the door weren't promising. But a car backing out of a spot at the far end of the lot seemed providential. He swung into the parking area and made a beeline for it.

The man behind the wheel of the departing car grinned and gave him a thumbs-up as he passed, and Craig waved in return. Claiming the spot, he set the brake and prepared to enjoy a rare high-fat, high-carb breakfast.

As he exited the car, he turned toward the restaurant—and came face-to-face with the *Lucy Sue* captain on the other side of the adjacent car.

Her sudden flush gave him the answer to his earlier question.

She'd bolted from the church to avoid him.

And she'd do it again if she could.

But there was no polite way to sidestep conversation with only the roof of a car separating them.

"Good morning, Kate."

"Lieutenant."

He dug deep for his most charming smile. The one he hadn't used in years. It felt stiff and rusty, like the hinges on a long unopened gate. "I thought we'd moved past the formalities."

"Sorry."

He waited, but when she didn't say anything else, he pocketed his keys and nodded toward the restaurant. "Indulging in a few treats?"

"Yes."

For a woman who'd had no trouble spewing out words in their previous encounters, her reticence bordered on alarming. "Is everything okay?"

Her color deepened. "Fine."

"Mommy, who is that man?"

Craig shifted to see through the windows of Kate's car. A little girl with long, raven-colored hair studied him through the glass, her expression curious, her dark eyes big in a face that seemed a bit too pale. She appeared to be about four or five.

The same age as Vicki.

The child's question loosened Kate's vocal cords. "That's the, uh, new lieutenant from the Coast Guard station, honey."

"You mean the invisible man?"

Once more, color flooded Kate's face. "Um…"

He called up a grin to put her at ease. "Don't worry. I've heard the moniker—and I'm trying to rectify it." He turned his attention to the little girl. "That's right. I'm the invisible man."

"You're not invisible now. I bet you were just too busy to come out before."

"I *have* been busy." He circled around the back of Kate's older-model Honda. The little girl was dressed in a plaid jumper with a red turtleneck sweater underneath, white tights, and shiny black shoes. Her hair was pulled back with a red ribbon, though a few wisps had escaped to form delicate waves around her face. She was a charmer.

As was her mother.

Kate had traded her work-worn jeans, slicker, and T-shirt for a slim black skirt, black pumps, and a long-sleeved green sweater the same hue as her irises. Her hair had been tamed with barrettes, one on each side, and lay soft on her shoulders. A touch of lipstick drew his attention to her mouth—and his pulse took a leap.

Not appropriate.

She was a married woman.

Crouching down, he focused on the girl. "My name's Craig. What's yours?"

"My real name is Madison, but everybody calls me Maddie."

"That's a very pretty name."

"Thank you." She gave him a shy smile and dipped her head.

"I see you're taking a few treats home." He tapped the white bag clutched in her hand.

"I ate one doughnut here. We sat on the bench over there so we wouldn't spill milk in the car or get sugar on the seats." She pointed across the parking lot toward the front door. "Mommy said I can eat the other one at home. Are you going to get a doughnut?"

"I might."

She leaned closer, her demeanor serious. "The sugar ones are best."

"I'll keep that in mind."

As Craig stood, Kate rummaged through her purse.

"I must have left my keys inside. Or on the bench." Giving up the search, she shook her head and inspected the shoulder-to-shoulder crowd, dismay tightening her features. "I guess we'll have to go back in."

"Maddie and I could wait here, if you'd like. It might be easier to get through the mob alone."

Her hesitation wasn't surprising. Despite his high-profile position, they were barely acquainted—and any decent mother would be cautious about leaving her child in the care of a strange man, no matter his pedigree.

He propped a hip on the back of her car and shoved his hands into his pockets. "You'll have a clear view of us, Kate. We'll stay right here."

She caught her lower lip between her teeth…then gave a quick nod. "Thanks. I'll be back in three minutes." She touched Maddie on the shoulder, the simple gold band on her left hand flashing in the sunlight. "Will you stay here with the lieutenant while I go find my keys?"

"Uh-huh."

After giving her daughter a scan—as if to satisfy herself the child wasn't going to freak out if she was left alone with a stranger—Kate plunged into the horde.

So where was her husband? Didn't he attend church—or could they be divorced?

He dipped his chin and regarded Maddie. She stood quietly beside him, her fingers crimped around the top of the white bag. He wouldn't probe. That would be wrong. But kids could be a fount of information.

He dropped down to her level again, staying behind the car so Kate could see him if she was keeping tabs. "Do you come here for doughnuts every Sunday, Maddie?"

"No. Just sometimes. I wish we could come every day, though. It's my favoritest place."

"I can understand that." He maintained a conversational tone—but up close, her pallor was more noticeable. Did she have health issues? Was that another reason for Kate's anxiety?

That question wasn't likely to be answered today. He only had three minutes, and they were ticking by fast.

"When I was little, there was an ice cream shop not too far from where I lived. That was *my* favorite place. In the summer, my daddy would take me and my mommy there after dinner. Like you come here."

Maddie's expression grew wistful. "I don't have a daddy. He died before I was borned."

Craig sucked in a breath.

Kate was a widow—and her husband had died while she was pregnant?

No wonder she seemed sad—and stressed.

When the silence lengthened, Maddie spoke again. "Do you have any little boys or girls, Lootenin?"

Uh oh.

How was he supposed to—

"I found them." Kate rejoined them, jingling the keys, then unlocked the car. "In you go, honey." She helped the child into her car seat, secured the straps, and shut the door. When she turned back to him, her expression was apologetic. "I overheard the end of that. Maddie has a tendency to give people the third degree—and she seems to have inherited her mother's bluntness.

43

I'm hoping it gives way to tact and discretion as she ages…unlike her mother's."

At her self-deprecating humor, Craig coaxed up the corners of his mouth. "I think I may have caught her mother on a couple of bad days."

Her eyes warmed a few degrees. "Thanks for cutting me some slack. And thanks for watching Maddie."

"My pleasure." His voice hoarsened, and he cleared his throat. "I'm glad you found your keys."

Their conversation was innocuous. The sudden sizzle of electricity between them wasn't.

Kate fumbled for the car door, slid in, and pulled it shut.

He stepped aside as she backed out and continued toward the restaurant.

End of story—except for one thing.

His pulse was pounding.

As he reached the door, he paused and looked back. Kate was watching him instead of the traffic on the road. As their gazes connected, she yanked hers away.

But unless his instincts were failing him, she was reeling from that electric moment too…and, like him, determined to ignore it.

* * *

"How's it coming, Chester?" Kate led Maddie through the gate in the tall privet hedge that separated her tiny back lawn from her neighbor's more spacious grounds and strolled over to the under-renovation guest cottage.

Chester set aside his paintbrush. "Hi, Kate. Good afternoon, Miss Maddie." He tipped an imaginary hat to the little girl, eliciting a giggle. "It's coming. A few more rain-free days like this, I'll wrap it up."

"I wouldn't count on Mother Nature's cooperation if I were you."

"We can hope, can't we? I don't know about you, but I'm ready for summer."

"After ten years, you ought to be used to Nantucket's long winters."

"Most days I am—though on cold, snowy ones Edith and I sometimes question our decision to retire here."

"I hear you—but when the sun shines and the sea sparkles and the sky is cobalt blue, this is a little piece of heaven."

"That's a fact." He swept a hand over the small outbuilding he was renovating for use as an efficiency cottage to rent to summer people. "What do you think?"

Kate gave it a once-over. "You're getting close."

"Not close enough to suit Edith."

Understandable. While she'd endorsed the idea when Chester had proposed it two years ago, Edith's enthusiasm had waned as he became distracted with other projects and the remodeling dragged on. The extra income she'd anticipated had never materialized.

"But you *are* making progress."

"Yep. Slow but sure."

Which about summed up his operating philosophy—in contrast to Edith, who bustled about, brimming with energy. How the two of them had ever gotten together was a mystery.

"Well, the tortoise did win the race."

"Tell that to my better half." Chester wiped his hands on a paint-smeared rag and examined his handiwork, a shock of gray hair falling over his forehead. "This will be a fine little hideaway.

Ideal for honeymooners who want privacy. I know Edith doesn't believe it'll be ready this season, but I'm determined to finish it. How's the *Lucy Sue* running?"

"So far, so good."

"Let me know if she needs any more adjustments."

"What would I do without you?" She leaned over and gave him a quick hug.

He flushed and shoved his fingers through his hair, wreaking havoc with the ornery cowlick no amount of hair gel could subdue. "You could turn a man's head with that kind of talk." Grinning, he inclined his head toward the house. "Edith call you over?"

"Mmm-hmm. She left a voicemail. Said she had a loaf of homemade pumpkin bread with my name on it." Translation? She had news to impart. The Nantucket *Inquirer and Mirror* had nothing on Edith Shaw when it came to scoops. Her neighbor had more connections than a Lego sculpture.

"That's what I figured. You go on in. She's probably champing at the bit. As for you, Miss Maddie, I know an old man who could use a helper for a few minutes."

Maddie's brow puckered, and she scanned the yard. "Where is he?"

Chester grinned. "Takes after her mother in the flattery department, I see. You're going to have to watch her with the gentlemen when she gets older." He took Maddie's hand. "So you don't think I'm old, hmm?"

As he led her daughter toward a toolbox on the other side of the small cottage, Kate crossed the yard and knocked on Edith's back door. Within seconds her neighbor pulled it open.

"What's this about pumpkin bread?" Kate stepped across the threshold and sniffed. The air was redolent with the aroma of cinnamon and cloves. "Mmm...it smells divine in here."

"My sentiments exactly." Heather Anderson, her other next-door neighbor, stepped out from behind the door.

"Taking the day off from The Devon Rose?" Not likely. The tearoom she'd opened on the first floor of her spacious house was popular with visitors and residents alike.

"I wish. I have a full house for afternoon tea. I just stopped over to return Edith's rolling pin. Mine broke in the middle of making scones. See you two later." She exited with a wave.

As the door closed behind her, Edith turned to Kate. "I have some news."

"I know. I got the message about the pumpkin bread."

"Pumpkin bread?" Edith's face went blank. "Oh, yes. The pumpkin bread. It's all wrapped and waiting for you." She waved a hand toward the counter. "This is more important than that. Guess who I ran into at Bartlett's Farm a little while ago?"

Considering that many of the islanders visited the upscale market and garden center on a regular basis, it could be anybody. "I have no idea."

"Lieutenant Cole." Edith beamed at her.

Oh, brother.

Her matchmaking neighbor had a one-track mind.

Kate sidled over to the counter to retrieve the pumpkin bread. "What a coincidence." She picked up the loaf and edged toward the door.

"Wait. There's more. He's available."

"For what?" Kate reached for the knob.

"You know perfectly well what I mean, Katherine MacDonald. He's not attached. The poor man lost his wife several years ago."

Kate dropped her hand. "He's a widower?"

"Yes. With a daughter. A four-year-old named Vicki."

Edith had reeled her in hook, line, and sinker.

Kate took a step back into the room. "She wasn't at church with him this morning."

"That's because she's staying with his mother in Wisconsin while he settles in. When I mentioned that I watch Maddie for you, he asked if I'd be willing to take Vicki too. He's got day care set up but would rather have her in a more personal setting. If you want my opinion, I think Maddie would benefit from a companion under the age of sixty. She spends way too many hours every day with me and Chester."

Kate frowned. "What did you tell him?"

"That I'd be happy to watch her, but that it was really your decision, since I committed to you first." Edith fished in the pocket of her skirt, pulled out a slip of paper, and handed it over. "That's the lieutenant's phone number. I told him I'd ask you to call him tonight so the two of you could discuss this."

Kate took the paper. "I don't know, Edith. Are you sure you're up to supervising two four-year-olds?"

The woman dismissed the concern with a wave. "I love children. The more the merrier. Besides, I suspect having two little ones will end up being less work for me. They can entertain each other."

It was hard to fault her neighbor's logic. And it would be wonderful for Maddie to have a child her own age to play with. Despite Lighthouse Lane's many charms, Maddie was by far the youngest resident. Plus, her daughter's asthma problem had kept her more confined than most youngsters her age.

The notion of contacting the lieutenant set off a flutter in the pit of her stomach—but if it helped Maddie, she could deal with a minor anxiety attack.

"I'll talk to him."

"Excellent. Worst case, we give it a try and it doesn't work. But I have a feeling everyone will benefit from this arrangement."

Kate shoved the slip of paper with his phone number into her pocket. "How so?"

"Maybe Maddie and Vicki won't be the only two to pair up."

Sheesh. Was nothing going to dissuade the woman from her newfound quest to find a suitable match for her widowed neighbor?

"Edith." Kate adopted her sternest expression. The one she used for unruly students at school. "Leave me out of the equation. Please. If you're so bent on matchmaking, why don't you push him in Heather's direction? She's single." Kate eased the door open.

"He's not the right man for her. Besides, she has no interest in romance."

"Neither do I."

"Baloney."

Kate huffed out a breath. "What's that supposed to mean?"

"Baloney. As in hogwash. My dear girl, you're a young and vibrant woman. You've mourned for four long years. You can't tell me you're not as lonely as that lieutenant has to be."

Her neighbor knew her too well.

Shoulders drooping, she opened the door. "I miss Mac, Edith. And yes, I get lonely. But one romance was enough. Mac was the only man for me." She took one step out the door. "Thanks again for this. Maddie and I will enjoy it." Without waiting for a response, she hurried away.

But as she collected her daughter and they walked home, Kate mulled over Edith's assessment of the new Coast Guard commander. Her neighbor could be right about Craig Cole being lonely. But that didn't mean he was interested in romance. There was a huge chasm between available and amenable.

And while she and the lieutenant both fell into the available camp, she'd be willing to bet he wasn't any closer to making the leap to amenable than she was.

5

S he was five minutes late.

Craig shifted in his seat at the small table in the café on Main Street, took a sip of coffee, and watched the front door. Kate hadn't sounded all that eager about meeting him for lunch when she'd called last night to discuss his day-care proposal—but after he'd told her there was more to the story than appeared on the surface, she'd relented and promised to meet him on his lunch hour.

Five more minutes passed.

Had she changed her mind?

While Edith had been agreeable to his proposal, perhaps Kate preferred for her daughter to have the older woman's undivided attention. Hard to blame her. But for Vicki's sake, it would be—

The front door opened, and a harried-looking Kate stepped over the threshold. Instead of her *Lucy Sue* attire of jeans and slicker, however, she wore black slacks, a green turtleneck sweater, and a black wool coat.

Craig stood, and she veered his direction.

"Sorry. I got delayed at school." She slipped into the chair he held, shrugging out of her coat.

"School?" He retook his seat.

"I sub at the high school. English, mostly."

"I thought you ran a charter business."

"I do—in season. During the off-season, I'm a substitute teacher. In case you haven't noticed, the cost of living on the island is high. It's tough to make ends meet with just seasonal work."

The waiter appeared as Craig digested this new piece of information. With two jobs, it was no wonder she often appeared tired—and stressed.

After Kate ordered a bowl of quahog chowder and he opted for a turkey sandwich, she got straight to business. "Tell me what it is we need to talk about that couldn't be discussed over the phone. I have to be back in forty-five minutes."

Despite his tension, a grin tugged at his lips. "Nothing like the direct approach."

She lifted one shoulder. "I don't believe in beating around the bush."

"I noticed." When a faint blush bloomed on her cheeks, he tried to mitigate any implied criticism. "And for the record, I prefer candor."

She acknowledged his caveat with a quick dip of her head and waited him out.

Craig took a sip of water. There wasn't any way to spin this that would put him in a favorable light, and his ego balked at admitting his failings as a father. But his pride was expendable. Vicki's welfare had to come first. He needed to suck it up and spit it out.

Psyching himself up for a tell-all session, he set the water glass back on the polished wooden table and folded his hands in front of him. "I assume Edith told you the basics. I'm a single parent, raising a four-year-old daughter."

"Yes."

"In our world today, my situation isn't unusual. But what led to it is." He clenched his fingers as his pulse began to hammer. "My wife and son were killed in a boating accident when I was stationed in Hawaii. It happened three years ago. Vicki was fourteen months old."

Shock rippled across her face. "I'm so sorry."

"Thanks." He took another sip of water. "Since then, Vicki has been cared for by nannies in the condo I rented in Washington. In the gap between nannies, my mother filled in."

"Edith said she lives in Wisconsin."

"Yes." Now came the hardest part. "In my grief, I shut myself off from Vicki. She has many of my wife's features, and whenever I looked at her she reminded me of all I'd lost. So I delegated her care to other people. Now, we have almost no connection. But I want to change that. A fresh start was one of my motives for coming to Nantucket."

"That sounds like a positive step."

"I hope so. I know it will be an uphill battle, but I want to give it my best shot. I don't intend to work the long hours I did in Washington, but I do need someone to watch her during the workday. I can go with the day care I have lined up if necessary, but I think she'd be happier with more personal attention from someone like Edith. And the icing on the cake would be Maddie. Vicki's never had a playmate, and having a friend her own age could help her adjust to her new environment. So I'm hoping you'll consider my request—for my daughter's sake."

Several beats of silence ticked by as Kate studied him. "I can see why you wanted to tell me your story in person. It's...persuasive."

"I hoped it would be." And there was more to it. But that could come later.

Maybe.

The waiter delivered their food, and after he left Kate let out a slow breath. "Let's give it a try. If the girls don't get along, or another problem arises, we can revisit the decision. Does that work for you?"

The tension in his shoulders eased. "Yes. And thank you. You have no idea how grateful I am."

Her expression softened. "I know how tough it is to be a single parent."

"Edith told me yesterday that you lost your husband." He stayed mum about the information he'd received from Maddie. "You've done a better job coping than I have. Maddie seems happy and well-adjusted."

"She knows she's loved. That makes all the difference."

His stomach knotted. "And that's where I've failed with Vicki."

"Grief can be destructive."

So could guilt.

But his spoken response was different. "You're cutting me too much slack. I was selfish and wrapped up in my own misery. That wasn't fair to Vicki. But I'm determined to do whatever I can to make things right with her…if she'll give me the chance."

"Children are forgiving creatures."

"I hope so. In fact, I'm counting on that." He motioned toward her bowl. "If you don't eat that, it will get cold."

She picked up her spoon. "When is Vicki coming?"

"I'm flying to Wisconsin to get her this weekend."

"So you'll need Edith starting a week from today?"

"Yes. I'll give her a call to finalize the arrangements."

They ate in silence as Craig racked his brain for an innocuous topic to fill the sudden quiet. Came up blank. Small talk didn't seem to fit their charged relationship.

In the end, Kate rescued him by spooning the last of her chowder into her mouth and reaching for her purse. "Sorry to eat and run, but it doesn't set the best example when the teachers are late."

A speck of the soup's cream base clung to the corner of her lips, and he tapped his own mouth. "A little misplaced quahog."

She wiped it off with her napkin—or tried to. "Gone?"

"Not quite."

She tried again.

He shook his head. "It's tenacious. Shall I?" He lifted his own unused napkin.

"Um...I guess. The kids would have a field day with this. Teacher with egg—or in this case, chowder—on her face."

He reached over and dispensed with the stubborn speck, her breath warm on his fingers. When his pulse picked up, he finished the job fast and tucked his napkin back on his lap. "Fixed."

"Thanks." Her response came out in a wheeze, as if the contact, however innocent, had goosed her pulse too. "I'll see you around."

Before he could stand, she took off.

He watched her until she disappeared out the door, then lifted his napkin. Faint traces of lipstick clung to it, left by a woman whose single-parenting skills far outranked his. Who knew that love made all the difference.

Love had once made all the difference in his life too, thanks to Nicole. Her sweet devotion had filled the place in his heart that had been empty for three long years.

The place that would *always* be empty, due to the part of the story he hadn't told Kate.

The part that proved he never deserved to love—or be loved—again.

Appetite disappearing, he wadded up the napkin, set it on the table, and rose, leaving the rest of his lunch—and any futile hopes of assuaging his loneliness—behind.

* * *

Kate took a discreet peek at her watch as Larry Atkins tried to move through the faculty meeting agenda at a brisk pace. But they'd gotten bogged down over a discussion about the deadline for final grades, and now she was late picking up Maddie. Edith wouldn't mind, but Maddie would. Her daughter usually watched for her at the window.

Of course, starting next week, she might be less anxious for her mother's return—assuming she got along with Craig's daughter. And why couldn't she, if the daughter was half as charming as the father?

Hard to believe that ten days ago she'd thought of the lieutenant as stuffy and arrogant. Their lunch today had been enlightening. It took courage—and humility—to admit your mistakes. That was admirable. As was his attempt to repair the damage to his relationship with his daughter. That spoke well of his character, and—

"Kate? Is that a possibility?"

At Larry's prompt, she pulled herself back to the meeting. All eyes were aimed at her. "Sorry. I, uh, missed the question."

"I was telling everyone that our speaker for the career assembly tomorrow bailed, and I asked if anyone knew of a possible replacement. Clarie mentioned she'd seen you at lunch today with the new Coast Guard commander. Would you be willing to ask him to fill in?"

Kate shot her coworker a disgruntled glare.

The other teacher sent her a silent apology.

"I don't know him well, Larry. Our few discussions have all been business-related."

The principal sighed and ran his fingers through his thinning hair. "We're in a bind here, Kate. I can do a cold call, but it would be less awkward for both parties if you put out a feeler. I could follow up with details if he's willing to consider it."

"It's very short notice." Considering how his simple touch of her lips with his napkin at lunch had disrupted her respiration, it would be safer if she walked a wide circle around him.

"But it can't hurt to ask. A lot of people in his position have canned speeches available for requests like this. It's just one phone call. I'll bring goodies from Downyflake to the teachers' lounge tomorrow if you'll do this."

A chorus of voices erupted, encouraging her to grant the principal's request.

"Fine. I'll call him." What else could she say? "But I'm not making any promises."

"Fair enough. Any other business?" When no one spoke, Larry ended the meeting. "I'll wait to hear from you, Kate. You have my home number if you don't reach him until later."

As the group dispersed, Clarie ambled over. "Sorry to put you on the spot, but I didn't think it would be a big deal. You two seemed pretty cozy." She leaned closer and lowered her voice. "So what's the scoop on your rendezvous?"

Kate stuffed her calendar and notebook into her satchel, twisted the latch, and stood. "There is no scoop. He wanted to talk to me about having Edith watch his daughter, like she watches Maddie. End of story."

The other woman's face fell. "He's married?"

For some reason, Clarie's disappointment rankled.

"Was. His wife died."

The other woman gaped at her. "Wow. What happened?"

"I didn't get any details." Kate edged toward the door.

"So you're not interested in him, right?"

Kate kept moving. "Right." She pushed through the door with more force than necessary.

Yet as it closed behind her and she went to make the call, she couldn't fault Clarie's interest. What available woman wouldn't want to be romanced by the tall, broad-shouldered lieutenant with the amazing blue eyes?

But she'd had her once-in-a-lifetime love—and no matter how appealing others might find the new Coast Guard commander, she was immune to his charms.

That little sizzle at lunch today, when he'd solved her quahog problem? An aberration.

Nothing more.

* * *

As she stood at the window of the teachers' lounge the next day, watching the relentless rain slash through the dreary landscape, Kate sighed and telegraphed a silent question to the gray heavens.

How come it's never easy, Lord?

No answer came.

None was expected.

God didn't answer questions like that with writing on the sky or in thunderbolts. It all came down to a matter of trust, of believing that all things worked together for good. She knew that. Accepted it.

But as far as she could see, there wasn't anything good in the sudden demise of the timing belt on her twelve-year-old Civic—and the accompanying several-hundred-dollar repair bill.

Why couldn't it have waited another six weeks to die?

She shoved her hands into the pockets of her slacks. Once the charter season kicked in, the cost wouldn't be such an issue—but her bank balance was often anemic by April. This year more than usual, courtesy of an extra trip to the pediatric pulmonologist and several high-priced tests and medications for Maddie. Her health insurance covered a chunk of those expenses—but not all. She'd be operating on fumes after this.

Thank heaven Chester had offered to do what he could when he'd dropped her off at school today—but she wasn't holding out much hope. While he was a great tinkerer, pulling off such a major repair would likely require more mechanical skills than he possessed.

Negative thinking, however, wasn't going to solve the problem. She'd find a way to deal with the unexpected expense, like she always did. Because moving away from the island, as her parents had been forced to do when the cost of living skyrocketed, wasn't an option.

"Hey, Kate, aren't you going to the assembly? After all, you got our speaker."

At Clarie's question, Kate turned her back on the bleak scene outside as two other teachers joined her in the lounge.

"My sole contribution was a thirty-second call. Larry took it from there."

"Personally, I can't imagine any available woman *not* going." Steph, who taught history, responded to Clarie's question as she rested her hand on the bulge in her tummy. "If I wasn't already spoken for, and motherhood wasn't imminent, I'd sit front and center. Did you get a load of that guy?"

"Yeah." Clarie gave an emphatic nod. "He is one hot dude!"

"I didn't know you ladies were talking about me." Hank Kraus pushed through the door with a grin. The social studies teacher smoothed down his thinning salt-and-pepper hair and patted his slight paunch.

"Cute, Hank." Clarie smirked at him. "We were talking about today's speaker for the career opportunities assembly."

"Oh, yeah. I saw him in the lobby. Impressive uniform."

"You're staying, aren't you?" Clarie aimed her query at Kate as she rummaged in her purse for her lipstick.

"For a few minutes. But I'm planning to sit in the back and sneak out early. I have to deal with car problems."

"I, for one, being available, interested, and attractive, intend to sit in the first row." Clarie applied her lipstick.

"Two out of three isn't bad." Hank ducked as Clarie aimed a playful jab toward his arm.

"I'll see you all at the presentation." Kate slipped out.

Ten minutes later, after a stop in the ladies' room to run a comb through her hair and touch up her own lipstick, she entered the auditorium. As she claimed the seat closest to the door in the last row, the principal strode onto the stage.

"Quiet, please. We're ready to begin." He waited until the teenage chatter died down before launching into his introduction. "Ladies and gentlemen, today we were supposed to wrap up our career series with a Navy pilot. Another assignment has kept him from joining us, but our new Coast Guard commander graciously agreed to step in. Some of you may have heard about his previous position at headquarters. But you may not be aware of the exciting life he led before he took a desk job in Washington. Today he's going to share with us some of his experiences as a Coast

Guard rescue swimmer. Please welcome Lieutenant Craig Cole."

As Craig rose from a seat in the first row, his dark blue dress uniform drawing attention to his broad, powerful shoulders, Kate stifled a groan. The man had been a rescue swimmer? A member of an elite group of well-trained men and women in superb condition who jumped out of helicopters into raging seas to save lives?

Why, oh why, had she hammered him about swimming off Great Point?

Kate sank lower in her seat and eyed the door. Could she sneak out?

Craig stepped behind the microphone and turned, displaying an imposing array of ribbons above his left pocket. He had a clear view of the door and would see her slinking out.

Too late.

She was stuck.

But once he began speaking, it didn't matter. Because he held every person in the auditorium—including her—spellbound with his stories of dramatic rescues in both the icy Arctic waters off Alaska, where he'd begun his career, and in the tropical seas off Hawaii, which held their own terrors for the unsuspecting.

Bottom line?

Craig Cole was a true hero.

Although he downplayed his role in the rescue operations he described, always giving credit to the entire Jayhawk team, when the flight mechanic gave the signal Craig was the one who'd jumped into the churning sea. This was a man who'd put his life on the line on numerous occasions to save others. He may have come to Nantucket from a desk job in Washington, but he'd earned his stripes the hard way.

Impressed didn't come close to describing her reaction.

Yet there was a disconnect.

In many of the rescue scenarios he'd described, Craig had talked about the need for flexibility, quick thinking, and improvisation. About the importance of modifying procedures to suit unique situations not covered by the rulebook. But since his arrival in Nantucket, he'd been hard-nosed about enforcing minor safety regulations. Everything had to be done precisely by the book, no matter the circumstances. She hadn't been his only victim.

It didn't make sense.

However, now wasn't the time to try and figure it out.

As he wrapped up his talk and a cluster of students surged forward to talk to him, Kate rose and slipped out the door.

Once she was a safe distance down the hall, she pulled out her cell and called Edith. The heavy rain would slow Chester down, but he'd arrive long before Craig finished answering questions from the enthralled students.

The call rolled to voicemail.

Crud.

She left a message, but tried again sixty seconds later.

Same result.

Kate tapped her foot. Worst case, she could duck into the ladies' room and wait for Edith's callback.

At least she wouldn't have to worry about running into the lieutenant there.

* * *

From his position in the front of the auditorium, surrounded by a large group of students clamoring for his attention, Craig caught a quick glimpse of fiery red hair disappearing through the rear door. Kate.

A wave of disappointment swept over him.

"Do you need to talk to Ms. MacDonald?"

The question from a gangly teen who'd noted Craig's line of sight refocused his attention.

"No. She seemed to be in a hurry."

"Yeah. She's got a lot on her plate. But she's never too busy to talk to the students or walk us through a tough assignment. She's awesome."

An apt description for a loving single mom, experienced charter fishing captain, and—judging by this student's evaluation—stellar teacher.

"Are there any women rescue swimmers, Lieutenant?"

The query from one of the girls forced him to switch gears. "Yes. A few."

For the next fifteen minutes he fielded questions, until the principal stepped forward and reminded the students their rides were waiting and that Craig had to get back to work.

"If any of you have other questions, give me a call at my office. I'll be happy to answer them." He withdrew a handful of business cards from his pocket and passed them around.

As the students broke up, he shook hands with the principal, accepted the man's thanks for being a last-minute substitute, and strode toward the door where Kate had disappeared. Maybe he could catch her.

But the hall was empty. She was gone.

Stifling a surge of disappointment, he pivoted toward the entrance.

"Lieutenant!"

He turned back. A thirty-something blonde flashed her teeth

and hurried toward him.

"I'm Clarie Peterson." She extended her hand. "I teach math here, and I wanted to say I enjoyed your talk. It was informative and inspiring."

"Thank you." He retrieved his hand with a gentle tug.

"Of course, I'm sure you barely scratched the surface in your presentation. I, for one, would be fascinated to hear more of your stories. I wondered if I might buy you a cup of coffee sometime?"

Keeping his PR persona in place, Craig searched for a diplomatic excuse to refuse. "I'm glad you enjoyed the presentation, Ms. Peterson. And that's a very kind offer. The thing is, I'm still learning the ropes at the station, and—"

The ladies' room door opened, and a pair of startled green eyes below a flaming halo of hair stared back at him.

Saved!

"Kate. I was hoping to catch you. Do you have a minute?" He telegraphed a silent SOS.

Her gaze flickered to Clarie. "Sure."

The blonde's eyes narrowed as she sized them up.

"Clarie!" Hank waved from down the hall. "We need to run or we'll be late for the get-together at Brotherhood."

"I'll be there in a sec." Clarie refocused on him and tossed her blond mane. "The offer of coffee stands. You can always reach me through the school. See you later, Kate."

Not until she disappeared around the corner did Craig speak. "Thank you."

Kate's lips quirked. "Clarie can come on a bit strong. She got divorced two years ago and lately she's been on the prowl. The pickings are somewhat limited, however, so when someone like you shows up..." She shook her head, and a faint hint of pink appeared on her cheeks. "A rescue swimmer, no less. I'm embarrassed about my faux pas at Great Point."

"Don't be. You were right. I took a foolish risk—and your dressing-down was a wake-up call. You'll be happy to know I've been more prudent in my swimming locations since then."

"Thanks for being gracious about it. Anyway, Clarie's a lovely person, if you're in the market."

"I'm not." Without giving Kate a chance to linger on that comment, he changed the subject. "The guy who called your friend mentioned a gathering. Am I keeping you from a social engagement?"

"No. I don't have the time—or patience—for small talk. Besides, I have to—" Her cell rang, and she retrieved it from her purse. "Would you excuse me for a second?"

"No problem."

As Craig listened to the one-sided conversation, it was clear Kate was relying on Chester to pick her up. He leaned over and spoke close to her ear. "Do you need a ride?"

She shot him a quick glance. Hesitated. "Can you hold a minute, Edith?" Pressing the mute button, she shook her head. "Thanks. I've got it covered."

"But I'm here. Chester's not. Why not save him a trip on this rainy day? Besides"—he gave her his most persuasive smile— "you rescued me a few minutes ago. One good turn deserves another."

As she studied him, Craig tried to hide his dismay at the impetuous invitation. Socializing with this appealing woman was dangerous.

Given how she caught her lower lip between her teeth, she was uncertain too. He ought to give her an opening to decline.

But he didn't.

After several more charged seconds, she spoke into the

phone. "Tell Chester he can stay dry, Edith. I have a ride." The slight quaver in her voice, however, suggested she was nervous.

And she wasn't alone.

6

Five minutes later, as Craig pulled up in front of the school and Kate dashed for his car, the word *mistake* kept repeating in her mind like a stuck needle on one of the old vinyl records her father used to play.

Spending time with the handsome lieutenant was *not* wise. With each encounter, his appeal grew—and that was scary. It could undermine her resolve to steer clear of romance. And that wouldn't be fair to Mac. When she'd given her husband her heart, it had been forever.

At least the ride to her house was short. She could steer the conversation to safe topics and make a fast escape the instant they arrived.

Craig stopped and pushed open the passenger door from inside.

Kate slid in. "What a day to forget my umbrella."

"Considering Nantucket's reputation as a resort destination, I have to admit I'm surprised by the weather."

"It's a *summer* resort—and around here, summer doesn't get a grip until June or July. The rest of the year can be like this. Or worse." She clicked her seat belt into place. "Take a right. It's not far." As he accelerated, she gave him a surreptitious scan. His medal-bedecked jacket was gone, replaced by a rugged, off-white fisherman sweater.

Catching her inspection, he grinned and answered her unspoken question. "I ditch the jacket as soon as possible after official functions. It's a high-maintenance garment. So, may I assume your need for a ride indicates car problems?"

"You may. My timing belt's shot."

He grimaced. "Ouch. That's an expensive repair."

"Tell me about it." Although she tried to keep her tone conversational, a subtle note of discouragement crept into her voice.

Of course Craig picked it up. "I suppose managing a budget with two seasonal careers has its challenges."

"That's a polite way to put it. Take a left at the next corner."

"Have you ever considered teaching full-time?"

"Yes. I was offered a position two years ago. But I'd lose two of my most lucrative fishing months—and it would almost be a wash income-wise. The group insurance premiums would be lower with teaching, but I like the flexibility of being available for Maddie." She sighed and shook her head. "There's no easy answer."

"I hear you."

"Take the next right. Then in two blocks make a left. I know the layout can be a maze to newcomers. The natives are used to it, though."

"How long has your family lived here?"

"Almost two hundred years. We go back to the whaling days. My ancestors did well on Nantucket, until kerosene and the Great Fire ended the glory days. Every generation since has had its struggles. Most of the family ended up moving to the mainland. It's tough for ordinary people to make a living on the island, especially in recent years."

"Any family still living here other than you?"

"No. Even my parents had to move. Several years ago they

sold the house where I grew up and relocated to a small bungalow in North Carolina." She swallowed past the sudden tightness in her throat. "They didn't transplant well. Two years later, my mother suffered a fatal stroke. Eight months after that, my dad died of a heart attack."

A few beats ticked by, and though she didn't turn her head, she could feel his gaze on her.

"I'm sorry. Back-to-back losses like that would be devastating."

"It was hard." Her voice hoarsened, and she swallowed. "Lighthouse Lane is the next street on the right."

He turned onto the tiny dead-end street containing a handful of houses, and she directed him to the small clapboard cottage tucked between two of the grander homes. "Thanks for the lift. I know Chester appreciates it as much as I do."

"It was my pleasure." He parked and shifted toward her as the rain continued to beat against the car, the rivulets of water acting like an opaque curtain, insulating them from the world.

His eyes warmed as he regarded her, and in the suddenly charged atmosphere her heart stuttered. The message he was sending, intentional or not, was clear. And scary.

She groped for the door handle. "Th-thanks again for the ride."

"Wait." His hand shot out, restraining her. "I have an umbrella in the back. No sense getting drenched. Let me walk you to the door." He retrieved it from the backseat, opened his door, and stepped out into the driving rain before she could protest.

While he circled the car, she tried to rein in her galloping pulse.

This was ridiculous.

She was not a teen with runaway hormones. She was a

mature adult—who was *not* interested in romance.

Period.

And she did her best to communicate that by keeping a discreet distance between them as they walked down the flagstone path that led across the tiny front lawn.

"I like your house."

She glanced at the weathered clapboard cottage, its sage-colored door and matching window frames giving the house a rustic charm in keeping with the historic nature of the town. Small as it was, it was chock-full of happy memories.

Many of them melancholy now.

"Thank you." While she dug in her satchel for her keys, he canted the umbrella over them. "The only thing missing is a porch or awning over the front door." And Mac, of course.

"I can see where that would be useful." A gust of wind sent a spray of water under the umbrella, despite his best effort to keep her dry.

She twisted the key in the lock. "Thank you again for the ride. I'm already late picking up Maddie—but not quite as late as I would have been if you hadn't come to my rescue."

"Is she at Edith's house?"

"Yes." Kate motioned toward the two-story Federal-style clapboard home to the left.

He scanned the yellow structure adorned with black shutters, which boasted a small set of friendship stairs at right angles to the front door that allowed visitors to approach the landing from either side. "Impressive."

"Compared to my house, yes. But not as grand as The Devon Rose." She motioned to the white, two-story clapboard house on the right that boasted black shutters, a Greek Revival roofline with a deep frieze, and a small, white-pillared front porch. "The owner lives on the second floor and serves afternoon tea downstairs." She twisted the knob and prepared to say goodbye.

"Would you like me to get Maddie for you? My giant umbrella will keep her dry. No sense having her catch a cold." A gust of wind spewed rain in their direction again, and he adjusted the angle of the umbrella to compensate. "And if you have an extra blanket, I could throw it over her as added protection."

Extending their contact wasn't smart from an emotional perspective—but it would be foolish to refuse his offer. Maddie already had more than her share of health issues, and a cold would only aggravate them.

"If you wouldn't mind, I'd appreciate it. Come in while I get an afghan." She pushed the door open, and Craig stepped inside behind her.

While she fetched the throw that was draped over the back of the sofa, he gave the spacious, open interior a slow scan.

"Wow. This isn't what I expected."

She picked up the afghan and faced him. "Everyone's surprised. We inherited the cottage from my husband's parents, who hadn't changed much through the years. The place was on the claustrophobic side. When we renovated, we followed the Historic District Commission guidelines outside—but tore down walls and took other liberties inside."

"I like the effect. It's warm and welcoming…and homey. You've managed to bring the house into the twentieth century without compromising the character of the original dwelling."

Yes, she had. *They* had.

She scanned the house she and Mac had worked on together, with its wide pine floorboards and exposed ceiling beams. Here at the front of the room, a cozy grouping of sofa and chairs clustered around the fireplace. Mac had painted the wooden mantel a

71

pale ochre, and an old-fashioned clock flanked by brass candlesticks stood in the center.

The dining space at the back of the room, defined by an area rug in a bold, contemporary pattern, was equally appealing. The sturdy wooden table, bare except for a fruit-filled lightship basket in the center and surrounded by four ladderback chairs with woven rush seats, had hosted many a happy meal. The cream-colored paint on the walls added to the feeling of airiness, as did the double French doors at the back that led outside.

"Thank you for the compliment. Mac and I worked hard to achieve that very effect."

"You also have excellent taste in art." He indicated the painting of Nantucket moors that hung over the mantel. "I noticed that the minute I entered. It's extraordinary."

"I agree." She gripped the top of the wing chair beside her and angled toward it. "My husband painted that."

Craig's eyebrows arched. "He was an artist?"

"Yes. He painted in the off-season, while I taught. He had the talent to do it year-round, but he liked the variety of two occupations. And he said being out on the water doing charters gave him ideas for paintings." She let out a slow breath. "I wish we'd kept more of his pieces."

"Did he sell at one of the local galleries?"

"Yes. As fast as he could paint them. I only have two." The fabric under her fingers rippled as she increased her pressure. "We both thought he had decades left to paint more."

"May I ask what happened to him?"

She took a long, slow breath. "He had an undiagnosed congenital heart defect. Hypertrophic cardiomyopathy, if you want the official name. It's caused by an asymmetrical thickening of the walls of the heart, and it can trigger sudden cardiac arrest. You mostly hear about it in athletes. But Mac liked to go scalloping with friends in the off-season, and that can be a pretty strenuous activity too. He was gone before they could get him back to shore."

A muscle clenched in Craig's jaw, and grooves appeared at the corners of his mouth. "I'm so sorry, Kate. I know that sounds trite, but there aren't any words that can comfort after a loss like that."

As he knew from personal experience, given the story he'd told her about his own losses.

"Thank you." She loosened her grip on the chair and smoothed out the wrinkled fabric. "Mac was only forty-one, with so much life still to live. I grieved for him, as well as myself. And for Maddie, who would never know her father. She was born two weeks after he died." She crossed to him and handed over the afghan. "I'll call Edith and let her know you're coming."

"That works." He tucked the throw under his arm. Hesitated, as if he was thinking about saying more.

But this wasn't a subject she wanted to talk about any further. She'd already shared more about it than she had with most people in her acquaintance.

"I'll light the gas logs while you're gone. It's an extravagance, but they always chase away the chill." She returned to the hearth and knelt by the fire.

Thankfully, he got her message. A few moments later, the door clicked shut behind him.

When he returned—after an absence long enough to convince Kate that Edith had chatted him up about his unexpected visit—she'd already made a cup of hot chocolate for Maddie.

From the small kitchen next to the eating area in the great room, she followed the sound of her daughter's giggles, pausing in the doorway.

Craig held Maddie in one arm, cuddling her daughter's delicate frame against his rugged sweater. The scene was the kind of father-daughter homecoming she'd always envisioned with Mac.

Her vision blurred, and she retreated a step, listening to their conversation as she tried to regain control of her emotions.

"I don't know." Craig's tone was serious, but there was a hint of teasing underneath. "I always heard little girls were made of sugar and spice. You could melt from all that rain."

More giggles. "Little girls don't melt."

"Are you sure?"

"Yes. I've been wet before."

"Well, I'm glad to hear that. I don't know what I'd tell your mommy if you dissolved into a gooey puddle."

Another eruption of giggles.

Lips bowing, Kate swiped the moisture from her lashes and stepped into the dining area.

Maddie's arms were still around Craig's neck, her cheek pressed against his sweater…and she didn't seem in any hurry to let go.

Neither did Craig.

He caught sight of her and grinned. "Here we are."

"So I see. Maddie, honey, I made you hot chocolate. It's in the kitchen."

"I like it here." She snuggled closer to Craig's shoulder.

Kate folded her arms as she met his gaze. "I think you've got a new friend."

"No complaints on my end. Want me to carry you into the

kitchen?" Craig directed the question to Maddie.

"Yes." She sniffled and wiped her nose on her sleeve. "Can you stay while I drink it?"

"Honey, I'm sure the lieutenant has to get back to work."

"To be honest, I'd planned to cut out after my talk today." Craig hitched up one side of his mouth. "That's a perk of being the boss."

Drat.

Edith was probably glued to the front window, waiting to see how long Craig stayed.

And the longer he hung around, the more difficult it would be to convince her matchmaking neighbor that his visit was nothing more than a simple ride home.

However, a sudden cough from Maddie erased any concerns about Edith. A minute ago her daughter had also sniffled. It could be nothing—yet after dealing with countless asthma attacks, she'd be foolish to overlook even the most innocent-appearing symptoms.

Yet being overprotective wasn't in Maddie's best interest, either. Best plan? Observe—and be prepared to act if necessary.

Putting on her cheerful face, she led the way toward the table. "I'll bring it in here for you instead. Craig, would you like a soft drink?"

"I'm a hot chocolate man, myself." He winked at Maddie again, eliciting another giggle.

As she prepared Craig's drink, her daughter coughed again—and Kate's stomach tightened into an all-too-familiar knot.

Please, Lord. Not tonight.

When Kate returned and set the two mugs on the table,

Maddie continued to jabber away while Craig gave her his full attention. But after another cough interrupted her chatter and her daughter wiped her nose again, Kate's concern escalated.

She took a seat, mind racing. What could have triggered an asthma attack today?

Nothing came to mind.

She'd kept Maddie out of the past week's cold air as much as possible, and when they *had* ventured out she'd had Maddie wear her special ski mask. Edith wouldn't have exposed her to any of the known triggers, either. Yet the sudden coughing and runny nose were suspicious.

As Maddie told Craig all about the pictures she'd drawn at Edith's while her mother was teaching, Kate leaned closer to her daughter and listened to her breathing.

What that a slight wheezing? Was she having difficulty—

"Mommy, aren't you going to answer the lootenin's question?"

Her daughter's query registered on a peripheral level as Kate faced the hard truth.

Maddie was definitely wheezing—and it was getting worse.

An asthma attack was imminent.

"I'm sorry…what did you ask?" Kate stood. How could she get the hated nebulizer ready without alarming Maddie? Even after three years of regular attacks, the episodes terrified her.

They terrified her mother too.

But unless she hid her own apprehension and kept her daughter calm, Maddie would panic—and hyperventilation would exacerbate an attack.

"Is there a problem?"

From the undercurrent in Craig's quiet question, he'd sensed her distress.

"Maddie, honey, can you finish your hot chocolate while the lieutenant helps me in the kitchen for a minute?"

"Uh-huh." She coughed and took another sip.

Craig frowned—but he rose and followed her in silence.

Once out of Maddie's view, she turned to him. "Maddie has asthma, and I'm seeing warning signs of an approaching attack. I have to give her a treatment and try to head it off." She crossed the kitchen and opened the door of a lower cabinet, hands trembling. As she withdrew the nebulizer, she spoke over her shoulder. "This isn't fun, Craig. You may want to head out before we get started. I'll explain to Maddie that you had to leave. It's okay."

And it was. It had to be.

Because it was her and Maddie against the world. The way it had always been. The way it would always be.

That was the reality.

Like it or not.

7

Kate could handle this crisis. Craig was certain of that, despite her white-knuckled grip on the machine she set on the counter, the slight quiver at the corner of her mouth, and her rigid posture.

She was a strong woman who was no doubt used to dealing with this situation alone.

But she didn't have to manage this one by herself.

"Why don't I help?"

She froze, and several beats of silence passed. "You don't have to do that." She kept her back to him, but it was impossible to miss the hint of longing in her voice.

"I want to. Tell me what to do."

A faint sound that could have been a sniff echoed in the quiet room. Then she straightened her shoulders and went back to work. "If you really want to stay, the best way you can help is to try to keep Maddie calm. She knows these spur-of-the-moment treatments mean an attack is probably coming."

"Any idea what triggered it?"

She shook her head as she washed her hands and began setting up the equipment. "I wish I did. I've been super careful about keeping her out of the cold and wind—and she knows to stay away from cats."

A cold knot formed in Craig's stomach. "What's the problem with cats?"

"She has a severe allergy to their dander, and allergies are huge asthma triggers."

Blast, blast, blast.

In one smooth motion Craig stripped off his sweater. Then he strode to the back door, opened it, and hurled the garment onto a sodden wooden bench a few feet away in the compact back yard.

When he turned back, Kate was staring at him as if he'd lost his mind, medicine in one hand, nebulizer cup in the other.

He blew out a breath and shoved his fingers through his hair. "I'm sorry, Kate. I'm the cause of Maddie's allergy attack."

"You have a cat?"

"No. But I was at my executive petty officer's house last night for dinner, and they do. His kids kept wanting me to pick them up, so I did—and I was wearing that sweater." He jerked his thumb over his shoulder, toward the back yard. "They played with the cat all evening."

Some of the color drained from her face, and she sped up her efforts to prepare the nebulizer, attaching the mask to a T-shaped elbow. "At least we're catching it early."

"Let me grab the afghan. It was up against my sweater." He retrieved it from the living room and held it up. "Where do you want this?"

"In the laundry basket. It's in that closet." She indicated a set of louvered doors at one end of the kitchen.

Craig deposited the blanket in the lidded container and rejoined her. "Do you want to do the treatment in here?"

"No. I sit on the couch and hold her. It helps keep her calm."

He moved to the sink and washed his hands, drying them on a paper towel. "Maybe I can distract her during the treatment. How long does it take?"

"About ten minutes."

"I finished my—" Maddie stopped in the doorway when she caught sight of the nebulizer. The rhythm of her breathing underwent an abrupt change, her deeper breaths giving way to shallow, quick puffs.

Craig moved beside her and dropped down to her level as she began to cough. Panic gripped her features, and he touched her cheek.

"Hey, sugar and spice. Your mommy thinks a treatment would help your breathing. Would you like me to tell you a story while you have it?"

No response.

Her attention was riveted on the machine.

Craig grasped her thin arms in a gentle grip. "Maddie?" He waited until she focused on him. "Would you like to hear a story during the treatment?"

She gave a jerky nod. "Can I sit...on your l-lap?"

"Fine by me, as long as your mom approves."

"That works." Kate finished the prep.

"Mommy, where's my...blanket?"

"I'll get it, honey. Craig, could you take her into the living room?"

After sweeping Maddie into his arms, he strode toward the couch and settled her on his lap.

Kate wasn't far behind. After handing a small, faded pink blanket to Maddie, she adjusted the mask on her daughter's face and turned on the compressor. "Sit up straight and take long, slow, deep breaths through your mouth, honey. That's it. Good girl."

Once Kate was satisfied with Maddie's inhalation, Craig launched into a tale about a rescue he'd participated in while stationed in Hawaii. It was one of his tamer stories, about saving a friendly Labrador, and he embellished it with as many colorful details as possible. Maddie clutched the blanket in one hand and clung to the sleeve of his dress shirt with the other, bunching the fabric in her fingers as she gave him her rapt attention. Kate knelt beside her, stroking her arm and murmuring encouragement.

When the cup containing the medicine was empty, Kate shut off the machine and removed the mask from Maddie's face. "That wasn't too bad, was it?" She took her daughter's hand.

"No." Maddie hiccupped and angled toward Craig, burrowing against his chest.

"Why don't you take a quick nap before dinner?"

"But we have company."

"Not for long." Craig stroked her hair. "I'm going home in a few minutes."

"Will you come with Mommy while she tucks me in?"

"If your mommy doesn't mind."

"That's fine. Come on, honey." Taking her hand, Kate led her down the hall that opened off the great room.

He trailed behind, past a bathroom on the right and a darkened room on the left, to the last door at the end of the hall. A Disney princess lamp on the bedside table bathed the small room in a comforting glow, and as Craig stepped inside he had a quick impression of pink walls, a woodland-fairy border, and white wicker furniture.

As he juxtaposed this room against the one he'd prepared for Vicki, his stomach dropped to his toes. His daughter's had no personality. No warmth. No...joy.

It was a disaster.

"Craig? What's wrong?"

He refocused on Kate. "I was thinking about the room I prepared for Vicki. It's...it needs work."

81

"Who's Vicki?"

"Vicki is the lieutenant's little girl." Kate aimed her next comment his direction. "I haven't told her about the arrangement yet."

"Sorry."

"No worries."

"You have a little girl?" Maddie's eyes rounded.

Kate sat beside Maddie. "It was going to be a surprise, honey. Vicki is the same age as you are. Mrs. Shaw is going to watch her every day too. So you'll have a friend."

Maddie's face brightened. "I always wanted a friend! When is she coming?"

"On Monday."

"What's wrong with her room?"

Craig rejoined the conversation. "I'm afraid I didn't know what little girls like. So it's kind of plain."

"We know what little girls like. We can help you fix it. Can't we, Mommy?"

It probably wasn't wise to set up another meeting with Kate, given the electricity zipping between them. But considering the sad state of Vicki's room, assistance from any source would be welcome—no matter the risk.

"I know you're busy, but to be honest, I could use all the help I can get. I want Vicki to feel welcome and wanted—and first impressions matter."

"I think we could squeeze in a quick shopping trip. Would tomorrow night work? We could meet you at your house to see the room, then go from there."

"I'd be forever in your debt."

"We'll make it real pretty for her." Maddie settled back on the pillows. "I'll think of all kinds of things for you to buy."

As Kate responded, she threw him a wry look. "Of that I have no doubt."

"Mommy, where's Raggedy Ann?"

"In my bedroom, honey. Remember, I was patching her arm? I'll get her for you."

As Kate left the room, Maddie whispered to Craig. "You have to get stuffed animals and dolls. And fairy-tale books and sparkly barrettes. And a bedspread with princesses and—"

"Maddie." Kate reentered the room and tucked the doll next to the little girl. "We'll talk about all this later, while we eat dinner. I want you to rest for a little while." She shook her head. "Like that's going to happen."

"See you tomorrow, Lootenin."

"Good night, Maddie. You keep thinking about things we should put on our shopping list."

"I will. Don't worry."

Stifling a smile, Craig exited into the hall while Kate lingered to turn off the bedside light and answer one more question from her daughter. As he strolled toward the living room, he glanced into the bedroom on his right. It was a simple but cozy room, dominated by a brass bed covered with an intricately patterned quilt in shades of green. An antique dry sink with an oval mirror stood against one wall, and a carved wooden rocking chair with a seat cushion occupied the far corner.

But it was the painting between a pair of windows that caught—and held—his attention.

Kate was front and center on the canvas, her lips tipped up in a Mona Lisa imitation, her glorious red hair dancing in the wind as she stood on the deck of the *Lucy Sue*. Her hands were propped on her waist, the worn denim of her jeans outlining her legs. She wore a cream-colored shirt, the cuffs of the long, full sleeves tight at her wrists. Backed by the white-capped cerulean sea and a cloudless blue sky, dominating the scene with a powerful presence, she again brought to mind the Irish chieftain pirate Grace O'Malley.

This had to be the other Mac MacDonald painting Kate had kept.

From her ready-to-take-on-the-world stance to the fire and passion glinting in her eyes to the energy and vitality radiating from her confident bearing, the painting captured every nuance of her personality. Her grit, determination, and strength. Her vibrancy and enthusiasm. Her deeply emotional, sometimes volatile, temperament.

This rendering depicted Kate in love. With the sea, with life—and with her husband.

It was masterful.

Kate reached past him, into the room, and flipped off the light. "Sorry to keep you waiting."

"No need to apologize." He motioned toward the darkened room. "That's quite a painting." Why pretend he hadn't noticed it?

"It was Mac's only portrait." She moved down the hall, her back to him.

"That's a shame. He had remarkable talent."

"I agree. But he claimed he only had one portrait in him. That subject matter was more his style." She waved a hand toward the panoramic scene over the fireplace as they entered.

"I suppose that could be true. Capturing people's personality may require a different talent than rendering a landscape. But he succeeded with yours."

"It's how he saw me, anyway." She swallowed and shoved her hands into her pockets. "Thanks for helping with the treatment."

"She seems to be fine now."

"She is—but the attack could escalate again later. We may be in for a long night."

"Has she always had asthma?"

"Yes, though it took a while for the doctors to settle on the diagnosis."

"And there's no cure?"

"No. We do the best we can to control it with medication. I'm hoping she outgrows it. My mom had it as a child, and it went away when she got older. Maddie's pulmonologist in Boston is optimistic she'll follow the same pattern."

Kate traveled to Boston because of Maddie's health issues? To see a pricey specialist, who no doubt ordered expensive tests and prescribed costly medications?

No wonder she struggled to make ends meet.

But it was easier now to understand why she preferred her flexible teaching schedule. While a full-time position would provide more financial security, it wouldn't give her the ability to be there for Maddie when the need arose.

"I can see how that would put a strain on finances."

She turned her head toward the fire, giving him a view of her pensive profile and the slender column of her neck. "You have to play the hand you're dealt. It's all about choices."

"Not everyone makes good ones." He raked his fingers through his hair. "Vicki suffered because I didn't. I have a lot to make up for with her—and I don't have a clue where to begin."

She turned back to him, the firelight casting a golden glow

on her fair skin. "Yes, you do. I've watched you with Maddie. You have a natural instinct with children. Maddie's shy with most people, but she connected with you immediately. Vicki will do the same if you follow your heart and love her. Love is a powerful healer."

Was it?

And if so, could love heal him too? Could it fill the dark, empty places in his heart and his soul?

Could a woman like Kate add new life to his days?

"Do you really believe that?" His gaze locked with hers.

Her sharp intake of breath was telling. "Are we still talking about Vicki?"

He could lie and say yes—but from what he'd seen, Kate appreciated honesty.

"No."

She eased behind a wing chair, keeping it between them. "In the right circumstances, I do believe love has the power to transform lives." She swallowed. "Pardon me if I'm reading too much into your reply, but in case you're interested in a short-fused charter fishing captain, you need to know she's not in the market for romance."

"Why not?"

"I loved Mac with every fiber of my being, and when he died, part of me died too. I can't risk going through that again."

"Because you're afraid?"

Twin furrows creased her brow. "I don't know that I'd call it fear."

"A rose by any other name…"

Her frown deepened. "Prudence is different than fear."

"It's a fine line."

"Have you crossed it?"

"What do you mean?"

"You've never remarried."

"Not because of fear."

"Then why?"

He studied her in silence for a moment...then called up every ounce of his courage and dredged up the words he'd spoken only in the quiet of his heart. "Because I don't deserve another chance."

She gave a slow blink. "I don't understand."

Starting this conversation had been a mistake—but it was too late to backtrack now. The door had been opened.

"Would you like to sit for a minute?" He motioned toward the couch in front of the fireplace.

She crossed to it and perched on one arm.

He followed more slowly and sat on the opposite side. Clasping his hands between his knees, he leaned forward and focused on the flickering flames. "You already know that my wife and son were killed in a boating accident in Hawaii three years ago. What you don't know is..." His heart began to hammer. "It was my fault."

In the silence that followed, he didn't have to see her face to know that shock had wiped the expression from it.

"I don't...that isn't...I can't reconcile that with the man I've come to know."

"It's true. If I'd been more diligent, my wife and son would be alive today."

"But...you're not the negligent type. If anything, you're *too* conscientious."

"Not that day. And all it takes is one slip to saddle you with a lifetime of regret."

"May I ask what happened?"

In his peripheral vision he saw her lean forward—but he couldn't make eye contact. Not until he got through this.

"The day it happened I was on duty in the search and rescue command center. I'd given up rescue swimming six years earlier, when Aaron was born, figuring it was too dangerous for a family man." He blew out a disgusted breath. "Ironic, isn't it? I gave up my risky job to protect myself from the sea, yet they were the ones the sea claimed."

"Were they swimming?"

"No. Sailing."

"Alone?"

"Yes. My wife was the daughter of a career Navy man, and she knew her way around boats and the ocean. She was more careful than I was. I never worried about their safety."

"What happened that day?"

"We'd had a report of minor seismic activity in the Aleutian Trench. Not sufficient to generate a tsunami warning, although we were watching it. I considered alerting Nicole, but she hadn't said anything about taking the boat out and I got busy. Didn't even bother to check my texts. Mistake number one."

He massaged his brow, then reclasped his hands. "To make matters worse, I'd taken the adult-size life jackets out of our sailboat the night before. I'd intended to replace them with new ones I planned to pick up on my way home from work. Again, I neglected to tell that to Nicole. Mistake number two."

He risked a peek at Kate.

Her gaze was riveted on him.

Focusing on the fire, he resumed his story. "Early that afternoon, we began getting calls about a moderate-size rogue wave offshore. Shortly after that, a report came in of a capsized pleasure boat. Our boat." His voice scratched, and he cleared his throat. "A rescue team was dispatched, but it was too late. Aaron had been trapped inside the cabin when the boat turtled. He was wearing his life jacket. Nicole had suffered a blow to the head, probably from the boom. Because of me, she didn't have a life jacket. They both drowned."

Only the steady ticking of the clock on the mantel broke the sudden, oppressive silence in the room.

At last, Kate emitted a shuddering sigh, and when she spoke her voice was laced with tears. "I can't begin to imagine what you went through."

A fresh wave of guilt and remorse slammed into him, and he had to force his lungs to inflate. "It was a taste of hell. But nothing less than I deserved."

When she didn't respond, he looked over at her.

Her brow puckered. "I'm not convinced that's true. The mistakes weren't all yours. If your son was wearing his life jacket, your wife must have known the adult jackets were missing before she left the dock. Besides, very few flotation devices will prevent an unconscious person from drowning."

"If Nicole was only dazed, it could have saved her. And if I'd read her text, told her about the seismic activity, she would never have gone out in the first place."

Kate caught her lower lip between her teeth, her expression pensive. "Now I understand the motivation behind your over-zealous safety program here. But you can't plan for every contingency. Life doesn't work that way." She leaned toward him, radiating compassion. "The accident was the result of a tragic sequence of events. No one would blame you."

"*I* blame me. And I'll carry that burden of guilt for the rest of my life."

"You could give it to God instead."

He shook his head at her gentle suggestion. "I know that's supposed to work in theory. But I've tried. It won't go away."

"Maybe the real problem is that you can't forgive yourself."

"Maybe." He drew a steadying breath and rose. Much as he'd like to stay here beside her and let the warmth of the fire—and her empathy—seep into his soul, he should go before he started down a beckoning road that would only lead to a dead end. "But I don't see that changing."

"That's a shame—for your sake, and Vicki's." She stood too. "Thank you again for your help with the asthma attack."

"I caused it."

"Not on purpose. Just like you didn't cause the boating accident on purpose."

"The consequences of that were tragic, though." He moved toward the door to retrieve his umbrella.

She stayed by the couch, bracing her hands behind her as she leaned on the back, oozing empathy and kindness. It was a different view of Kate than the one Mac had painted, but it was equally powerful...and true...and appealing.

He fiddled with the umbrella. "Is the offer of help with Vicki's room still on the table?"

"Of course. Does six o'clock work?"

"Yes." He twisted the doorknob. "I hope you have a quiet night."

"So do I. Drive safe."

The rain continued to beat a staccato rhythm on the pavement as he stepped outside, and Craig dipped his head against the onslaught as he jogged toward the car.

Once behind the wheel, he glanced back toward the golden light spilling from the windows of Kate's small cottage—where he'd felt so at home. Far more so than in his sterile, rented condo in Washington or the house he now occupied that felt more like a hotel than a home.

But he needed to make it one—for Vicki's sake. And he needed to create a family, even if it was never more than the two of them.

Strange.

Two weeks ago that had seemed like an overwhelming task. Far more intimidating than any of the dangerous, roiling seas he'd dropped into during his days as a rescue swimmer.

Yet thanks to a feisty charter captain and her charming daughter, he no longer felt adrift. Kate and Maddie were living proof that two people could be a family. And with their assistance—and their example to follow—perhaps he could give Vicki the kind of loving home she deserved.

That was at least one optimistic note on which to end the day.

Yet as he put the car in gear and drove down Lighthouse Lane, his trepidation escalated again.

Because life—like the sea—was rarely placid for long.

8

"Pathetic, isn't it?"

At Craig's question, Kate scanned Vicki's spartan bedroom.

A matching white headboard, small dresser, and nightstand were set atop a bland beige carpet. Utilitarian mini blinds hung at the two windows. A navy blue blanket covered the twin bed, which had been made with military precision. The walls were white and bare, the top of the dresser empty. A brass lamp stood on the nightstand.

The only youthful touch was a lonesome teddy bear that rested against the white case of the pillow on the bed.

As she tried to come up with a diplomatic comment, her daughter stepped in with a pithy assessment.

"Yuck."

"Maddie!" She swung toward her. "That's not polite."

"But it's true." Craig sent the little girl a reassuring smile and reached out to lay a hand on her shoulder. "Thank you for being honest. So where do we start?"

Kate dragged her gaze away from the muscular forearms below the rolled-up sleeves of his cotton shirt and pulled a tape measure out of her purse. "Let's get the dimensions of the windows."

"I can do that. Without a ladder, too." He plucked the

measuring tape from her hand, the brush of his fingers against hers sending a tingle all the way to her toes.

And setting off all kinds of alarm bells.

Kate took a discreet step back and dug in her purse for a notebook. "If you'll read off the measurements, I'll jot them down."

Once that task was accomplished, she tucked the notebook back into her purse. "I think we can do this in two or three stops. How do you feel about painting?"

"On a scale of one to ten—two. But I don't mind wielding a brush for a couple of hours if you think that will help. What color did you have in mind?"

"Pink." Maddie's tone was definitive. "That's the bestest color."

"Pink it is, then. Shall we, ladies?"

As they exited the room, Maddie tugged on Kate's hand. "I have to go potty, Mommy."

"First door on the right." Craig pointed to it. "I'll wait for you in the kitchen."

Maddie kept up a running commentary as she used the bathroom and washed her hands. When she finished, Kate opened the door—and Maddie headed in the wrong direction.

"Wrong way, honey." She took off after her and folded the little girl's hand in hers. "It's easy to get confused in a new place."

"It's kind of a big house, isn't it?"

"Yes." Compared to their snug cottage, anyway.

"Is that the lootenin's room?" Maddie stopped outside a room illuminated by a muted light.

Kate peeked in. This room featured a queen-size bed—also neatly made—and was unadorned too…except for a photo of a family group on the dresser. A younger Craig had his arm around a blond-haired woman, while a little boy with brown hair grinned back at the camera from between them.

"I guess it is, honey." She urged Maddie down the hall. "If we don't hurry, bedtime will come before we can visit all the stores."

Craig was waiting for them in the kitchen, as promised. He'd donned a dark brown leather flight jacket, and he reached for Maddie's coat as they approached.

While he helped her daughter slip her arms in and button up, Kate shrugged into her own quilted jacket and surveyed the kitchen. An empty can of soup stood on the counter by the sink, and a package of bagels rested next to a toaster. No other food was visible.

"If you're wondering, I did stock up on kid-friendly fare."

The man had an amazing ability to read minds. "Kids can be kind of picky eaters."

"I figured that." He secured the last button on Maddie's coat and stood. "I got peanut butter and jelly, white bread, cereal, hot dogs, pizza, and ready-to-nuke chicken strips. Not the healthiest menu...but I didn't think tofu or arugula would cut it—and I'm not certain of her preferences."

"Wow!" Maddie gaped up at him. "You did real good on the food part, Lootenin."

"Kid pleasers, no question about it," Kate agreed. "You may want to have fresh fruit on hand too."

"Pineapple," Maddie offered. "And strawberries."

"Duly noted. Shall we?" He motioned toward the door, and they set off.

For the next two hours, Kate hustled them from store to store, selecting a self-stick woodland-fairy border with matching curtains and comforter, pink sheets, a lamp with a whimsical winged fairy seated on a toadstool, a small combination toy chest/bookshelf with books and toys to go with it, and two colorful posters. At Maddie's suggestion, Craig added a stuffed pink unicorn with a sparkly mane.

On the practical front, Kate also helped him pick out a car seat, like the one they'd transferred from her car to his for the evening excursion with Maddie.

When their shopping spree was finished and they returned to his house, Kate left a sleeping Maddie in the car while the two of them carried in his purchases. Then Craig moved Maddie, car seat and all, back to Kate's car. After shutting the back door, he joined her on the driver's side as tendrils of fog began to swirl around them.

"Will you be okay driving home?"

"I've been all over this island in much worse conditions— and I don't have far to go." She tossed her purse onto the passenger-side seat, fighting back an urge to find an excuse to extend the evening. But it was late, Maddie was tired, and she had a full teaching day tomorrow. "However, when fog rolls in, it's best to reach your destination ASAP."

"Makes sense." Yet he didn't move from beside her car— and in the sudden silence, her pulse picked up. Unless she was mistaken, he was as reluctant to end this interlude as she was. "Listen…I really appreciate your help. The stuff you found— Vicki will love the room."

"I had fun tonight."

He hitched up one side of his mouth. "Spending other people's money can be quite a kick."

"That wasn't why I had fun." As the clarification spilled out, she stifled a groan. Comments like that were *not* going to keep the commander at arm's length should he start to have any romantic leanings. A fast exit was in order. "I should be—"

"Wait." All traces of levity had vanished from his face, and his eyes had darkened. "I feel the same way. It's been years since family-type activities were part of my life. Tonight brought back happy memories."

Pressure built in her throat. "For me too."

Somewhere in the distance, a boat whistle echoed in the fog. A long, plaintive sound that brought to mind lost souls seeking safe harbor. Searching for peace and rest and safety.

Just as she—and the island's new Coast Guard commander—were.

Both of them had sustained gut-wrenching losses and struggled to deal with the aftermath of tragedy. And both had reconciled themselves to life without a mate.

She'd been fine with that. Resigned to her single status.

Until the man standing inches away from her had walked into her life.

Or, more accurately, until she'd stormed into his.

As the fog intensified, cutting them off from the rest of the world, Craig shifted closer—until no more than a whisper separated them.

Though the night was chilly and the undulating gray mist damp, the air between them was heated—and filled with temptation.

The leather of Craig's jacket chafed as he lifted his arm, and an instant later his fingers connected with her cheek.

A rush of longing rocked her, unbalancing her as effectively as a stormy sea beneath the *Lucy Sue*.

Sweet mercy.

He was going to kiss her.

And she wanted him to. More than was wise. So much that

if she didn't leave this instant, her shaky self-control might shatter.

Jerking back, she jammed her key in the lock. "I have to go."

"Kate…I'm sorry. I didn't mean to overstep."

At the distress in his voice, she forced herself to take a calming breath and meet his gaze. The yearning she'd spied moments ago had been replaced by contrition.

"It's not a problem." Even if her shaky voice suggested otherwise. "Let's just chalk up what happened to two lonely people caught up in the spell of remembering happier days—and wishing they could return."

Though it had been more than that for her.

And for him, unless her instincts were malfunctioning.

But thankfully, he didn't press the issue.

"Be careful going home."

"I will. Have a safe trip to Wisconsin." She slid behind the wheel, and he shut her door.

As Kate eased out of his driveway and pulled onto the street, she allowed herself a quick peek back.

He was standing where she'd left him—but as she drove away, he disappeared into the mist.

Unfortunately, the aftereffects of their near-kiss didn't. Her nerve endings continued to vibrate, and the surge of longing his touch had evoked hadn't yet dissipated.

What was going on?

She hadn't kissed a man since Mac died. Hadn't even *considered* kissing a man. Any man, let alone one she'd met less than two weeks ago.

While the explanation she'd given Craig was plausible, it didn't account for all the other occasions an image of the broad-shouldered Coast Guard commander had flashed through her mind, distracting her from whatever she was trying to do—grade papers, fix dinner, balance her checkbook.

Bottom line, the man had gotten under her skin.

And as she drove through the thickening mist that was obscuring all the comforting landmarks of her familiar world, she hadn't a clue how she was going to deal with it.

* * *

At the knock on her back door Friday night, Kate pulled the last plate from the dishwasher, wiped her hands on a towel, and moved across the kitchen.

"Is Mrs. Shaw bringing us a treat?" Maddie stopped coloring, her expression hopeful.

"How do you know it's Mrs. Shaw?"

"Only the Shaws come to our back door. And Mr. Shaw's favorite TV program is on tonight."

Impressive deductive reasoning for a four-year-old. "Maybe."

But if her neighbor *was* bearing food, it meant she was either hunting for information or had news to impart. And lately, a handsome lieutenant had been high on her list of newsworthy topics.

Kate braced and pulled the door open.

Yep. It was Edith. And the plate of oatmeal cookies in her hand confirmed the purpose of her visit. No doubt prompted by the mass of damp wool dangling from the woman's other hand.

Drat.

How could she have forgotten about Craig hurling his sweater into the backyard the night of Maddie's asthma attack?

"I found this on your bench." Edith inclined her head toward the knitted garment.

"That's the lootenin's." Maddie peeked under Kate's arm.

Edith arched an eyebrow.

"It's, uh, kind of a long story." Kate scrubbed her palm on the denim of her jeans.

"I don't have any pressing matters waiting at home."

Of course not.

"Would you like to come in?"

"Yes. A visit would be wonderful. What do you want me to do with this?" She hefted the sweater.

"Leave it out there. I'll deal with it later."

Dropping it on the chair beside her, Edith handed Kate the plate of cookies and stepped inside. "These came out of the oven five minutes ago."

"Thanks for thinking of us. Go ahead and hang your coat on a peg. And please wash your hands." Kate spoke over her shoulder as she carried the plate into the dining area.

"I washed them before I left the house."

"That sweater you picked up had a close encounter with a *c-a-t*."

"Ah." Edith moved to the sink and turned on the water. "That explains it."

She was drying her hands as Kate came back in. After pouring two mugs of coffee, Kate handed her one and filled a glass with milk for Maddie, who'd already planted herself beside the plate of cookies.

"These smell yummy, Mrs. Shaw." Maddie's voice drifted in from the dining area.

"Let's sample them, by all means." The older woman claimed a seat at the table, broke off a bite of cookie, and popped it in her mouth. "Not bad, if I do say so myself." She brushed off her fingers and addressed Kate. "You told me about the episode Tuesday night, but not the cause."

She should have expected that lapse to come back and haunt her. Very little got by Edith.

"Are you talking about my asthma attack?" Maddie took another cookie.

Or her daughter.

"Yes, honey." Kate perused the plate of cookies and selected one as she responded to Edith's comment. "I didn't mention the cause because I didn't want to embarrass him—or make him feel worse than he already did about the feline issue."

"The lootenin stayed for my treatment. He told me a story." Maddie continued to chow down on cookies. "It was fun while he was here."

"I'll bet." Edith stirred some cream into her coffee, acting altogether too pleased. "What a delightful picture of domesticity."

"And Mommy and me went to his house to see Vicki's bedroom. It was yucky." Maddie wrinkled her nose. "But we went to the store with him and bought all kinds of stuff to fix it up. Maybe we can go see it after it's done." Maddie's face brightened. "Can we, Mommy?"

"I don't know if we'll be invited back, Maddie. And you'll see Vicki every day at Mrs. Shaw's."

"But not the lootenin."

Edith jumped back into the conversation. "I can remedy that. I called him earlier today and invited the two of them for dinner Sunday night when they get back from Wisconsin. I came over to invite you both to come too. I thought it would be helpful for the girls to get to know each other with their parents present rather than being thrown together as strangers on Monday morning."

Excitement sparked from Maddie. "Can we, Mommy?"

Kate hesitated. After their unsettling parting on Tuesday, another encounter close on its heels might not be wise. Yet her neighbor's rationale was sound. A casual dinner in Edith's home would familiarize Vicki with both the setting and her caregiver. And it would also give the girls an opportunity to get comfortable with each other.

No logical excuse to refuse came to mind—and she didn't intend to share the illogical ones with Edith.

She was stuck.

Judging by the older woman's smug demeanor, the Lighthouse Lane matchmaker knew that.

Kate threw in the towel. "Count us in. Can I bring anything?"

Edith shook her head and rose. "Just your appetite. That's what I told Craig too." She leaned over to kiss Maddie's forehead. "I'll see you both at church. Would you like to ride with us this week, Kate?"

"Sure. Thanks."

"Can we go to Downyflake afterward?" Maddie chimed in. "We could celebrate my new friend."

"Celebrating new friends." Edith gave a satisfied nod. "I like that. Excellent idea, Maddie. After all, a person can never have too many friends." She aimed the last remark at Kate before she trotted to the door. "I'll let myself out."

As her neighbor exited, there was no mistaking the meaning behind *that* comment.

Edith wasn't about to abandon her matchmaking mission for the foreseeable future.

God help them all.

* * *

Less than three hours into his reunion with his daughter, Craig was having serious qualms about his ability to win her over.

As his mother refilled his coffee cup on Saturday night, Vicki scrutinized him from the other side of the table—just as she'd been doing since his arrival. Usually with a solemn expression while gripping his mother's skirt.

Not that he blamed her for her clinginess. Her grandmother had been the most constant loving presence in her young life. But her dubious appraisal was unnerving. It was clear his daughter didn't feel any more confident about his fathering abilities than he did.

"Are you ready for pie?"

At his mom's question, he forced himself to shift gears. "Are you kidding? I've been salivating ever since I saw it on the counter." In truth, his appetite had vanished. But Lillian Cole was an excellent cook, and she'd gone to a great deal of effort to prepare an excellent dinner. "After all that fried chicken, though, I should resist. Pretty soon I'll need Roto-Rooter to clean out my arteries."

She gave him a playful nudge as she picked up his plate. "You don't have to worry. I've been eating fried chicken and apple pie for most of my seventy years and my cholesterol is well within the normal range. I gave you stellar genes." She picked up Vicki's almost-untouched plate. "Are you finished, honey?"

The little girl nodded and tightened her grip on the ragged yellow blanket she'd been carrying around with her since his arrival.

It reminded him of the one Maddie had.

"Would you like a piece of pie, Vicki?"

"Can I have ice cream instead?"

"Of course. One extra-large scoop of vanilla coming up. Shall I add a little chocolate sauce?"

"Uh-huh." Vicki sent a big-eyed, forlorn stare his direction.

The knot in his stomach tightened another notch.

While his mother did her best to keep a lighthearted conversation flowing during dessert, his daughter answered in monosyllables. And when he mentioned getting ready for bed, she wanted nothing to do with him, despite her grandmother's urging to let him handle the chore.

Craig had long ago learned to deal with rejection—but coming from his daughter?

Different story.

His mother telegraphed him an apology. "Would you like to come along, Craig?"

At his daughter's crestfallen expression, he shook his head. "No. You two go ahead. I'll handle KP."

Vicki left the kitchen without even saying good night.

Despite the churning in his stomach, he dived into the cleanup—and tried not to think too far ahead.

But tomorrow night, when it would be just him and Vicki, loomed ominously.

In the past, the nanny had taken care of the bedtime ritual, often long before he got home from the office. And in the morning, he'd been gone before his daughter woke up. It had been easier that way. Less painful.

For him, anyway.

The problem was, he'd realized too late how much he'd

alienated his daughter and abdicated his responsibilities as a father—and he'd had no idea how to repair the damage.

He still didn't.

But he had to try. He owed it to Nicole...and Vicki...and himself.

So now, together on Nantucket, they'd sink or swim.

"She's all settled." His mother reentered the kitchen and pulled out a mug for tea. "Don't take the rejection personally, Craig."

He stood with his back to the counter and pressed his palms flat behind him, gripping the edge. "How else am I supposed to take it?"

She slid the cup of water into the microwave and pressed a button. "She doesn't know you. The awkwardness will dissipate when it's just the two of you."

"I wish I could believe that."

"Believe it. You were a wonderful father to Aaron—and to Vicki when she was a baby. Those skills are still there."

Were they?

Maybe.

Maddie had responded to him, after all.

But she was a happy child who'd always been loved and cherished. And she knew it—because Kate lavished her with love and attention.

Vicki, on the other hand, had no memory of a doting parent. Nicole had died when she was fourteen months old, and he'd been emotionally absent since then. She presented a far bigger challenge than Kate's daughter.

"You seem doubtful."

At his mother's comment, Craig tightened his grip on the edge of the counter. "I am. In terms of Vicki, anyway." He exhaled. "She might be little, but she knows I haven't been there for her. She doesn't trust me. Rightfully so. And I don't know how to deal with that."

"By loving her. By being there for her from now on. By taking charge of her care instead of passing it off to a nanny. By doing exactly what you're doing right now. You'll win her over, Craig. I have every confidence that in six months you two will be the best of buddies. And I'll be praying for that."

So would he.

Because he was going to need all the help he could get to make the two of them a family.

9

When Edith opened the door the next night to admit them, the headband sporting two playful daffodils that bobbed on gold coils above her head provided welcome comic relief after a tense trip.

"I like your headpiece." Craig forced up the corners of his mouth. "It's very...festive."

"Thanks. I'm getting in the mood for the Daffodil Festival. Only two weeks to go, you know. And our three million daffodils are determined to arrive on schedule. I did a drive-by along Milestone Road today. Pepped me up after our long winter." She bent down to his daughter. "You must be Vicki."

His daughter edged closer to him. No more than a hair—but he'd take it. She'd kept her distance during the entire trip, saying little, just watching him with those big, solemn blue eyes.

He dropped down to her level, her grip as firm as ever on the tattered blanket she'd insisted on holding during the entire trip. "This is Mrs. Shaw, Vicki. The lady I told you about, who's going to take care of you while I'm at work."

"And we're going to have such fun." Edith bent down. "Do you like to bake?"

"I don't know how. But sometimes I helped my grandma."

"Wonderful! I can always use an experienced helper.

Tomorrow we'll make chocolate chip cookies. Do you like those?"

Vicki nodded.

"I thought you might. Come on in. Kate and Maddie are already here."

As he stepped inside, Craig gave the interior a scan. The cozy Early American décor suited the hospitable manner of the owners.

But he was more interested in the red-haired woman and dark-eyed little girl who stood waiting for them in the living room. At Kate's smile, some of his tension dissipated.

"Now that we're all here, I have an activity for the girls." Edith opened a drawer in the antique sideboard along one wall and withdrew two coloring books, along with a pack of crayons. "Would you like to color until dinner?"

"I would." Maddie spoke up without hesitation and moved toward the older woman, giving Vicki a shy peek.

His daughter didn't respond.

Craig once again dropped to the balls of his feet beside her. "Do you like to color, Vicki?"

"Yes." She peeked at Maddie. "But I don't know her."

"I told you about her on the plane, remember? Mrs. Shaw takes care of her too. She's been waiting to meet you."

When Vicki hesitated, Kate joined them. "Hello, Vicki. I'm Maddie's mommy. Your daddy told me all about you and how happy he is you're coming to live with him. Maddie's been so excited. She hopes you'll be friends."

"I've never had a friend."

At Vicki's muted reply, Kate's eyes softened. "Well, we're going to fix that. You'll have lots of friends here."

The little girl eased closer to her. "Are you the one who helped my daddy fix my new room?"

"Yes."

"It's pretty. Pink is my favorite color."

"Maddie picked it out. That's her favorite color too." Kate motioned her daughter over and took her hand. "Vicki likes pink too, honey."

"I knew you would." Maddie edged closer. "My room isn't pink, but I have a bunch of pink stuff in it. Maybe you can see it sometime. Could she, Mommy?"

"I don't see why not." Kate took the second coloring book from Edith and began to flip through it. "What would you like to color, Vicki?"

The little girl tucked herself in beside Kate, watching as she turned the pages. "That one." She pointed to a picture of a family sitting on the ground, enjoying a picnic.

"I like that one too." Maddie leaned over Kate's shoulder on the other side.

"I wish I had a family like that."

His daughter's wistful tone tugged at Craig's heart.

"Me too. I only have a mommy. My daddy went to heaven," Maddie told Vicki.

"My mommy went to heaven." Vicki continued to focus on the picture of the family.

"But you have a nice daddy."

Vicki's skepticism was obvious, but before she could give voice to it Edith herded the girls toward the kitchen table. Chester, wearing a daffodil boutonniere and a grin, took up the rear.

"Thanks for smoothing out the intros." Craig stood and extended a hand to Kate.

She took it as she rose, her fingers warm in his. "She's a darling girl."

"But too quiet."

A burst of childish laughter came from the kitchen, and Kate's lips bowed. "I don't think that's going to last for long."

Craig shoved his hands into his pockets. "I hope not. The bedroom was a hit, by the way. She was thrilled."

"I'm glad." She hesitated, as if debating whether to say more—then continued. "Listen, if there's anything I can do to help ease this transition, let me know. Being a single parent is tough under the best of circumstances, but you've got an even bigger challenge to overcome. So if you ever want to talk or bounce ideas off someone, I'm available."

That was unexpected—but welcome. Since leaving his mother behind and boarding the plane with Vicki, he'd felt as adrift as a rudderless ship on a choppy sea.

"I appreciate the offer—and I may take you up on it."

Edith returned then, and for the remainder of the evening they had no chance to talk one-on-one as they downed pizza and the daffodil-shaped sugar cookies the older woman had baked for the occasion. But his heart was lighter as the get-together ended.

And he wasn't the only one who had been uplifted and encouraged. As he and Vicki walked toward his car, she was much more talkative.

"I like Maddie."

"I do too." He buckled his daughter into the safety harness. "She's a nice girl."

"Her mommy's also nice."

"Yes, she is."

"But Maddie wishes she had a daddy. Just like I wish I had

109

a mommy." Vicki emitted a quivery sigh. "Why do mommies and daddies have to die?"

An excellent question.

Too bad he didn't have an answer for Vicki…or himself.

"I don't know." He framed his reply with care. "Only God knows that. I guess he wants some of them in heaven with him sooner than we'd like."

She squished her blanket in her hands, holding it close to her chest as she regarded him in the dim light. "Are you going to die?"

At her tremulous question, his stomach clenched, and he touched her small hand with a finger that wasn't quite steady.

"God decides that, Vicki. But I'm going to do my best to be here for you. I want to take you to kindergarten on your first day of school. I want to help you learn how to read. And I want to go bike riding and swimming and fishing with you. How does that sound?"

"Okay." He started to back out of the car, but she grasped the edge of his jacket. "Will you tuck me in tonight and read me a story, like Grandma always does?"

"You bet. And I plan to do that every night from now on." He stroked her hair and shut the door.

So far, so good.

Nevertheless, Kate's offer to help if problems arose was a lifeline he'd keep close at hand.

Because every instinct in his body told him it was only a matter of time before he found himself in deep water—and sinking fast.

* * *

Of all the rotten luck.

As Kate secured the last mooring line to a cleat on the finger pier, she surveyed the *Lucy Sue.*

Courtesy of Chester, the engine was purring along. The teak trim was pristine. And she'd defy anyone to find fault with the deck after her liberal applications of elbow grease.

The problem lay under the water.

After a close encounter with a wayward piece of flotsam on her way back from Great Point, her propeller now had a sizable ding.

Translation?

A big-bucks repair.

She blew out a breath and propped her fists on her hips.

Once the charter season kicked in, the cost wouldn't be such an issue. But with the bluefish still making their way back to Nantucket from the warmer Florida waters where they wintered, it would be four or five more weeks before there were sufficient quantities of them to interest visitors in a fishing outing.

After giving the hitch knot one final tug, she shoved her hands into the pockets of her slicker and trudged down Straight Wharf and onto Main Street through the steady drizzle, debating her options.

"Kate!"

The familiar baritone voice jerked her out of her reverie, and she lifted her head, pulse accelerating. She may not have run into Craig since the pizza party at Edith's four days ago, but he'd made regular appearances in her thoughts.

As he waved at her from his car and slowed to a crawl, she picked up her pace.

"Sorry if I startled you." His brow knitted as she drew close. "Is there a problem?"

"I just dinged my propeller."

"How bad is it?"

"Bad enough. She's running rough."

"What happened?"

"I hit something out by Great Point."

"Ouch."

"I'll say—and my pocketbook will agree." The rain intensified, and she flipped up the hood on her slicker. "You should go. You're holding up traffic."

He glanced in his rearview mirror. "I only see one vehicle, and it's a block away. Where are you going?"

"Home."

"Where's your car?"

"Also home. I usually walk to the wharf." A gust of wind whipped past, flapping her slicker, and she dipped her head.

"Not the best idea today. You'll get drenched. Hop in and I'll give you a lift."

"I'm used to walking in worse weather than this. Besides, I don't want to take you away from your work."

He hitched up one side of his mouth. "To be honest, I'm happy to have an excuse to ditch my afternoon plans. I was going to visit the LORAN station, but I'm not keen on driving all the way to 'Sconset in this weather."

Understandable. The seven-mile-trip to the tower for the Coast Guard's Long Range Navigation station at the far eastern end of the island would be slow and tedious for a newcomer— especially if fog rolled in on the small coast-hugging road at the end, as it was apt to do.

Another blast of wind whipped past, and Kate capitulated. "In that case, I accept. Thanks."

She circled the car and slid in as he opened the door for her from the inside.

"Despite that slicker, you would have been soaked within a block."

"True. Your timing was impeccable." She pushed back her hood and tried to finger-comb her hair. Gave up. Damp weather always frizzed her fiery locks. "Lost cause. Bad hair days are my lot in life."

When he didn't respond, she turned to find him giving her an appreciative perusal. Seriously? How in the world could he find anything in her bedraggled state appealing?

Yet Mac had often worn that same expression. Even on days when her appearance was a wreck, he'd always seen past the ex-ternals and loved her for what was on the inside.

Loved.

The word sent a ripple of alarm through her, and she tucked her hand in her lap. A distraction was in order.

"So, uh, how are you doing with Vicki?"

Taking her cue, he turned his attention back to the road and eased the car over the uneven cobblestones at a slow crawl. "Bet-ter than I expected. She doesn't talk much, but she's eating. And she loves going to Edith's. Actually, I'm glad I ran into you. I was going to call in a day or two anyway. In case you haven't noticed, she and Maddie have become fast friends."

"I've noticed. That's all Maddie talks about."

"Since this is her first weekend here, I wondered if we could set up a play date. I have to confess I haven't a clue how to keep her entertained for two whole days on my own."

"It isn't necessary to entertain children every minute."

"I know. But until she settles in, I want to engage with her as much as possible. Though I could use a break for a couple of hours over the weekend. If you approve, I could take them both home with me after church and drop Maddie off at your house later in the afternoon."

"That would work. And if you don't have dinner plans for that night, why don't you stay and eat with us?" As the impromptu invitation popped out of her mouth, she frowned.

Where had *that* come from?

Craig's arched eyebrows suggested he was as surprised as she was—but it didn't stop him from accepting. "That would be great. I'm trying to add variety to our menu, but I've existed on frozen dinners for so long that any kitchen skills I once had are long gone. Macaroni and cheese pushes my abilities to the limit—and I think Vicki will get tired of that fast. We've had it twice already."

Her lips twitched. "I'm not promising a gourmet dinner, but I can guarantee it won't be macaroni and cheese."

"Sold."

He pulled up in front of her house, and Kate reached for the handle of the door. Best to make a fast exit, after the previous drop-off scenario.

"Let me get that for you." He started to open his own door.

"No!" Kate shoved the door open with more force than necessary, tamping down a jolt of panic as she moderated her tone. "No sense in you getting wet too. Thanks for the ride." She slid out, bracing herself as a gust of wind buffeted her. "I'll see you Sunday."

With that she shut the door, dashed for the house, and slid the key in the lock. Once inside, she leaned back against the door, heart pounding, and exhaled.

This was ridiculous. She was acting like a schoolgirl with her first crush.

Huffing out a breath, she strode into the living room. She had to calm down before she retrieved Maddie—and her favorite chill-out spot was the place to do that.

After flopping into the overstuffed, chintz-covered chair, she let her head drop to the cushioned back and focused on the painting above the mantel. Usually, the serenity of the timeless, windswept moors and distant sea in the scene seeped into her soul.

Not today.

Nor did the ticking of the clock that had belonged to Mac's great-grandfather soothe her. The antique piece had sat on this mantel for more than forty years, placed there the day Mac's parents moved into this house. And when she and Mac had inherited it eight years ago, after Mac's father died, the clock had remained. To her, it had always represented roots and stability and permanence.

All the things Kate was trying to hang on to in the face of her financial challenges.

But now she was facing a new risk. One that no infusion of cash would mitigate.

And Craig Cole was to blame.

The man was worming his way into her heart.

Kate massaged her temple.

In three weeks, he'd managed to turn her world upside down by reminding her what it felt like to be a woman, not just a mom. Forced her to confront the deep-seated loneliness that had drained much of the joy from her life. Made her yearn for things she'd never expected to have again. Companionship. Partnership. Love.

None of which made sense. She still loved Mac. Still felt connected to him. Still missed him.

How was it possible to have such strong feelings for a man

she'd known less than a month?

How was it possible to have such strong feelings for *any* man, after loving Mac?

She rose and began to pace.

Whatever her feelings for Craig, there was no point dwelling on them. He'd been clear that romance wasn't in his plans.

And if that happened to change?

Another formidable hurdle loomed.

Fear.

Loving carried the risk of soul-numbing heartache. If Maddie hadn't given her a reason to carry on after Mac died, she could have succumbed to the blackness that had tried to suck her down to a place she never, ever wanted to go again. A place from which even her strong faith hadn't been able to protect her.

While living the rest of her life alone wasn't an appealing prospect, neither was the risk of another devastating loss.

And as she psyched herself up to retrieve Maddie, she faced the simple truth.

A stumbling block of that magnitude could be impossible to overcome.

10

"Cross your fingers and let's see if we can add one more to top off this incredible castle." As the two little girls seated on the living room floor beside him watched, Craig added a final block to the tower.

The column wavered.

The girls gasped.

The tower steadied.

Sighs of relief.

"Wow. That's the tallest castle I've ever built." Maddie regarded it in awe.

"Yeah," Vicki seconded.

His cell began to ring in the kitchen, and Craig extricated himself from the pile of blocks around him. "You girls can build the wall around it while I answer that."

As they set about the task with vigor, his lips tipped up. All that worry about how to entertain the two of them for several hours had been wasted. Their active imaginations had filled in the gaps.

The phone continued to ring, and he picked up his pace. Could it be Kate, touching base to verify everything was under control?

But the woman's voice that greeted him didn't belong to the charter fishing captain.

"Hi, Mom. Is everything okay?"

"Why do you ask me that whenever I call?"

"Habit, I suppose." One formed after his dad died seven years ago, when concern about his mother living alone in the house his parents had shared for thirty-five years weighed on him. But Lillian Cole had done fine, proving eminently capable of managing her solo life.

"You should break that one. I'm right as rain, like always. How's everything going there?"

"Not bad—so far."

Childish giggles erupted from the living room, followed by the sound of tumbling blocks.

So much for his castle.

"Are there children at your house?"

"Kudos on your hearing, Mom."

"I may be getting old, but all the parts still work. Does Vicki have a playmate?"

"It's the other little girl from the day-care situation I arranged. They've become great friends already."

"Excellent. A companion her own age will do wonders for Vicki. And speaking of companions…I have a bit of exciting news. Brace yourself—I'm getting married."

Silent seconds ticked by as he tried to process that bombshell.

"I got the same reaction from your brother." His mother sounded amused.

Craig managed to locate his voice. "Why didn't you tell me last week, while I was there?"

"Because he just proposed last night."

"I assume Harold is the groom?"

"Who else? He's a fine man, Craig. You'll like him once you get to know him."

"I already like him, Mom." Harold Simmons, with his shock of white hair and British accent, appeared to be a true gentleman.

"Glad to hear it. To tell you the truth, I'm still adjusting to the notion of being a bride again at my age. But how can you fight fate? If Harold hadn't moved into town to be near his daughter and grandchildren, then bought that small bookstore, we'd never have met."

"I agree it seems providential."

"The perfect word. I went in to buy a book, ended up staying for tea—and the rest is history. Sometimes, when you least expect it, God steers you into the path of the ideal companion."

An image of Kate flashed through his mind—but he tried to squelch it. His mom's news deserved his full attention.

"When's the wedding?"

"Next month, if we can pull it off. On Nantucket—if possible. I've heard it's a beautiful place, and with you there and Steve in New York, it would be a convenient location for our family. Harold's daughter doesn't mind traveling there for the ceremony. She says it would be a great excuse for a vacation."

"You're not wasting any time, are you?"

"At our age, there's not much time to waste. Why wait?"

"I can't argue with that. What can I do to help?"

"Shall I read you my whole list now, or give it to you in small chunks?"

At her teasing tone, his lips curved up. "Hit me with all of it."

"Let's start with the minister. Can you recommend someone?"

"You'd like the pastor at the church I'm attending, and I'm

sure he'd be happy to perform the ceremony. The church itself is lovely too."

"To be honest, Harold and I would prefer to get married in a natural setting. We've both done the big church wedding. And I know the Lord will be with us whether we're in his house or his backyard. We also want to arrange a small, simple reception. And Harold and I will need somewhere to stay for a week. I hoped you might be able to recommend someone familiar with the island who could help me pull all the pieces together. I could hire a wedding planner, but that feels a bit impersonal."

Kate came to mind at once. She knew all the ins and outs of the island. But she was also a single mom with two seasonal jobs who didn't have a minute to call her own as it was. It wouldn't be fair to ask her to get involved in coordinating an event like this.

"Let me think about it, Mom. I'll also talk to Reverend Kaizer and get back to you later in the week. What day did you have in mind for the ceremony?"

"We were hoping for Monday, May twenty-second. We could all fly in over the weekend and get settled. Plus, Monday should be a quieter day on the island. Given the short notice, that may open a few more options in terms of venues."

"True." Craig jotted down the date. "Anything else?"

She snorted. "Isn't that enough for one day?"

"More than. I'll be back in touch soon. And Mom...I'm happy for you."

"Thank you, dear. To be honest, it's been kind of a whirlwind. I thought my life was fine as it was. But in hindsight, it was like the days I work late in my garden, not even noticing how dim the world has grown until I step inside, flip on a light, and realize I'd been in the shadows. That's what Harold did for me. He flipped on the light in my life again. And I pray every day that someone new will come along for you too."

Once again, an image of Kate flashed through Craig's mind. And once again, he stifled it. "I appreciate the thought, Mom. But don't hold your breath. I'm not planning another foray into matrimony."

"I wasn't, either. It was God's idea. And his plans don't always mesh with ours, as I discovered. Just be open to them, son—and don't rule anything out."

His mother's advice echoing in his mind, Craig said goodbye and ambled back to the living room. The two little girls were engrossed in their make-believe castle game, creating worlds where heroic knights on white chargers slew dragons and lived happily ever after with the fair maidens they rescued. No shadows darkened their idyllic existence.

But there were plenty of shadows in real life. And heroes tended to have feet of clay.

Nevertheless—was there anything wrong with wishing God would answer his mother's prayers and help him find a way to give his own life a happily ever after?

* * *

"That was the bestest chocolate cake I ever ate." Vicki swiped at her mouth with a paper napkin, managing to smear the icing rather than remove it.

"I second that." Craig leaned over to wipe the excess off her chin.

"The spaghetti was real good too." Maddie speared the last bite of her cake.

"I second that as well." Craig took a sip of coffee and sent

Kate a smile that turned her insides to mush.

Enough of that.

She rose and began to clear the table.

"Let me help."

Before she could protest, Craig stood too and picked up the girls' plates.

"Mommy, can me and Vicki play in my room?"

"Sure."

The two girls scampered off.

As Kate led the way into the small kitchen, the youngsters' chatter drifted down the hall from Maddie's room.

"She's a different girl with Maddie." Craig paused in the doorway, listening to the animated exchange between the girls. "I haven't managed to elicit that kind of enthusiasm from her yet."

His wistful tone tugged at Kate's heart. "Give her time."

"You sound like my mother." He deposited the plates on the counter. "I had a piece of surprising news from her today, by the way. She called to say—"

A knock sounded at Kate's back door, and she wiped her hands on a dish towel as she moved toward it. "Don't lose your train of thought."

"Sorry to bother you when you have company, Kate." Edith peered over her shoulder as soon as she opened the door and waved at Craig. "But this came for you yesterday while you were out and Chester forgot to bring it over. I had a feeling you might be waiting for it." She handed Kate an overnight package.

"Thanks. I was." Kate took the bulky envelope and set it on the kitchen table as Edith followed her in. No doubt her neighbor had been delighted to have an excuse to scope out the dinner party next door.

"I hope I didn't interrupt anything." The expectant look

Edith gave them said otherwise.

"No. We're finished with dinner." Craig leaned back against the counter and crossed his arms. "I was getting ready to share a piece of news with Kate."

"Oh?" Edith's expression morphed to curious.

"I had a call from my mother this afternoon. She's getting married."

"A wedding!" Edith clasped her hands. "Isn't that romantic?"

"I guess so." One side of Craig's mouth quirked up. "But it's hard to think about my mom in that light."

Edith raised an eyebrow. "I'll have you know that romance knows no age limits, young man. When's the big day?"

"She's hoping for May twenty-second. And they want to have the wedding here—outdoors, if possible. I'm supposed to arrange everything with Reverend Kaizer."

"What about a reception?"

"I'm supposed to find someone to arrange that too."

"Hmm." Edith cocked her head. "Will this be a small wedding?"

"Very. No more than fifteen people."

"I'll tell you what. If you think your mother would be interested, I'd be happy to coordinate everything on this end."

Kate shot her a suspicious glance.

Edith ignored it.

"Are you serious?" Craig seemed as surprised by the offer as Kate was. "Despite the small size, it will still be a lot of work."

Edith waved his comment aside. "I don't mind in the least. Why don't you discuss it with your mother, and if she's agreeable, have her give me a call."

"I'll do that. Thank you."

"My pleasure." She squinted at her watch. "Gotta run. There's a program on public TV tonight that Chester and I want to catch. Enjoy your evening." She hurried through the door, pulling it shut behind her.

"Wow." Craig shook his head. "Is she always such a go-getter?"

"Yes." Especially when she was on a mission—whatever it was. "And she'll do a terrific job. She's a past president of the garden club, and under her supervision we had some of the best Daffodil Festivals ever. Plus, she knows everybody on the island. Count your blessings for the offer."

"I'm counting my blessings on many fronts these days."

Electricity began to ping around the room as his husky comment hung in the air, and she angled away to wipe down the counter. "It, uh, may be wise to take a peek at the girls. It's gotten kind of quiet in there."

A few beats ticked by.

"Right. I'm on it."

Kate let out a slow breath as he disappeared down the hall.

At least he hadn't followed up on that charged remark.

But perhaps she'd read too much into it. After all, hadn't he told her he had no interest in romance? Hadn't she told him the same thing?

Yes and yes.

She hadn't imagined the electricity, though. It was still vibrating in her nerve endings.

And try as she might, she couldn't stifle the tiny flame of hope that suddenly flickered to life in her heart.

* * *

As Craig reached the end of the story Maddie had asked him to read to the girls, he slowed his pace.

He needed a bit more space from the lovely woman who was fast undermining his conviction that he didn't deserve a second chance at love.

But even if he could get past the guilt, the situation with Kate was complicated. She earned her living on the sea—the same sea that had robbed him of his wife and son. A relationship with her would carry risks. Big risks. Wouldn't it be testing fate to take that kind of gamble?

Yet now that she'd brightened his life, chased away the shadows his mother had talked about, how would he ever find the strength to cope with the endless parade of solitary months and years stretching ahead?

"You have to read the last line, Lootenin. That's the best part."

At Maddie's comment, Craig refocused on the book in his hands. The last line was the standard fairy-tale ending.

"And they lived happily ever after."

The very ending he'd always yearned for.

But in his experience, happy endings were the stuff of dreams, not reality.

"Will you read us another one, Lootenin?"

At Maddie's question, he shook his head. "Not tonight. Vicki and I have to go home now."

"Can't we stay longer?" His daughter inched closer to Maddie. "I like it here."

So did he.

"You'll see Maddie tomorrow, at Mrs. Shaw's."

"I guess." She crawled across Maddie's bed and slid off, reaching for the tattered blanket that was never more than an arm's length away.

Craig took her hand and led her down the hall, Maddie trailing at their heels.

He stopped at the kitchen doorway, and Kate turned to them. For an instant, a flash of—disappointment?—strobed through her eyes. But she quickly masked her reaction.

"Heading home?"

"Yes. Thank you for a wonderful dinner."

"Thank *you* for arranging the play date. I was able to get a ton of work done."

"Did you go down to the *Lucy Sue?*"

"No." She indicated the package Edith had delivered. "In my spare time I do freelance book editing for a publisher in New York. A friend of mine had a connection there and got me in. It'll never make me rich, but it's a welcome supplement to my income and the hours are flexible. I work on the manuscripts at night, after Maddie's in bed."

So Kate had *three* jobs.

Which was consistent with what she'd told him early on—that despite the financial pressures weighing her down, she intended to stay on the island. And she was doing everything possible to make that happen.

Sweet mercy, this woman was strong. More than strong, in fact. She was a survivor. The kind of woman who fought on through discouragement—and kept fighting until every last piece of ammunition was gone.

"You're amazing." The comment slipped out before he could stop it.

A faint blush stained her cheeks. "Stubborn is more like it."

"I stand by what I said. But I do have one question. When do you sleep?"

"Quality is more important than quantity—and knowing I'm solvent leads to more restful sleep."

"What's solvent?"

At Maddie's question, Kate redirected her attention to her daughter. "Um...it has different meanings for different people, honey. For me, it means happy."

"Oh. I guess I'm solvent too, then."

Craig reined in a chuckle. "Nice save."

Kate flashed him a quick smile. "Let me get your coats."

After retrieving them, she helped Vicki zip hers up while Craig slid his arms into his leather jacket. They followed her to the door, and she opened it. Stepped back with one hand still on the knob, the other resting on Maddie's shoulder. "I think it's going to rain again. Drive safe."

He ought to leave.

But he didn't want to.

Just say good night and get out of here, Cole.

Sound advice. He should listen to it.

Yet how could he ignore the yearning in Kate's emerald eyes...or her softly parted lips...or the call of her satiny smooth skin as the golden light on the hall table spilled across her cheeks, warming her complexion and gilding her hair?

It would take a man with superhuman powers to resist the unspoken invitation she was sending.

He wasn't that man.

Following his instincts, he leaned close enough to catch the faint, pleasing fragrance that was all Kate. Brushed a kiss against the gentle curve of her cheek. "Good night, Kate."

She didn't respond.

Not in words, anyway.

But her sudden, shallow breathing...and the pulse beating in the hollow of her throat...spoke volumes.

Leave, Cole. Now. Before the temptation to give her a real *kiss is too strong to resist.*

Summoning up every ounce of his willpower, he took Vicki's hand and led her through the night toward their car, putting distance between him and the woman who was fast invading his heart.

But physical distance wasn't going to solve his problem.

Because that simple touch of lips to cheek had left him wanting more.

Much more.

And he had no idea what to do about that.

* * *

Sleep was not going to come.

Staring at the ceiling in her dark room, Kate lifted her hand and pressed her fingers to the spot Craig had kissed on her cheek. Drew in a long, slow breath.

It did nothing to quiet her restlessness.

Heaving a sigh, she shoved back the covers. May as well get up until she was more in the mood for slumber.

After donning her robe, she padded down the hall to the living room and flipped on a light. Crossed to the sofa and sat, tucking her legs under her as she focused on Mac's painting, letting its quiet beauty seep into her soul.

Her husband had been blessed with an incredible talent—and this sensitive rendering embodied that gift. It reflected the soul of a man in love with life. A man who'd been able to find beauty in unexpected places and whose masterful skill had allowed others to see the world as he saw it. A man who'd always seized opportunities for joy, who'd believed in the heart's infinite capacity to love.

Of all people, Mac would understand that nothing could ever diminish what they'd shared. The man who'd stolen her heart and filled her days with sunshine and beauty and grace, who'd taught her that life was to be embraced, would understand that the part of herself she'd given to him would be his, and his alone, for always. And he would want her to move on. To love again if the opportunity came along.

She knew that now, with absolute clarity.

But the fear of loving—and losing—remained. Craig appeared to be healthy and vibrant, but Mac had exuded vigor too. Yet, as she'd learned, life didn't come with guarantees—at any age. And living with that constant worry would be hard. So very hard.

The clock on the mantel began to intone the hour, twelve steady, predictable bongs echoing in the quiet room. A room where she ended each day the same way.

Alone.

And lonely.

But perhaps God was offering her an opportunity to change that if she could find the courage to open herself to love. To encourage the interest Craig had displayed tonight.

However—while her parched heart yearned for love, much as the plants in her garden needed the restoring rain the approaching storm would bring, her self-preservation instincts were strong.

What a conundrum.

And she'd find no answer to her dilemma tonight.

She'd also be a basket case tomorrow if she didn't get at least a few hours of shut-eye.

Kate rose and pushed herself to her feet, sending a silent plea heavenward as she retraced her steps down the hall.

For guidance...and wisdom...and the courage to embrace the future she was meant to have—whatever that might be.

11

Craig emptied his pockets of change and set the coins on the dresser in his room as a yawn sneaked up on him.

What a day.

As hectic as it had been at the station, the stress level at home had been even higher. But in light of her missed nap and her friend's asthma attack this afternoon, it wasn't surprising that Vicki had picked at her dinner, balked at taking a bath, and turned thumbs down on all the books he'd suggested as a bedtime story.

Edith had warned him that Vicki had been upset by the incident, but she'd wanted nothing to do with the subject when he'd broached it at dinner, closing up as tight as a Nantucket quahog.

It seemed for every step forward he took with her, they regressed two steps.

Expelling a breath, he picked up the photo on his dresser and ran a finger over the smooth koa-wood frame, a familiar pang echoing in his heart as he studied the four-by-six snapshot that had been taken on a weekend trip to Volcanoes National Park on the Big Island a couple of years before the tragic accident. The dramatic, black lava rock had provided a superlative backdrop for their laughing, animated faces, offering a sharp contrast to Aaron's light brown hair and Nicole's long, wavy blond mane.

Pressure built behind his eyes, and he gritted his teeth. Getting emotional, giving in to grief, wouldn't change his reality. He had to—

"Daddy?"

At Vicki's tentative question, he jerked toward her. She was standing two feet away, clutching an empty plastic cup, her ratty blanket trailing behind her.

Swallowing past the lump in his throat, he returned the photo to the dresser. "Do you need water?"

She nodded.

"Coming right up." He took the cup from her.

She didn't follow him to the kitchen, so after he filled the glass he started back down the hall, toward her room.

Except she wasn't there.

He continued to his room, where he found her contemplating the photo on his dresser.

"I have your water, Vicki. You can drink it in your room."

She spoke without turning. "Where's me?"

Her plaintive, forlorn question twisted his gut.

He set the glass on the chest next to the door and joined her. "That was taken before you were born, honey."

A few seconds of silence ticked by as she inspected it. "How come it makes you sad?"

She must have been watching him longer than he'd thought. "Because I miss them."

"Would you miss me if I was gone?"

At her wistful tone, his vision misted. "Of course I would."

"But how would you remember me?"

For such a tiny thing, she could sure rip the heart out of him.

"You're right. I need more photos. I'll tell you what. Tomorrow, we'll start taking pictures of us together. Would you like that?"

She examined the photo again—but asked another question instead of answering his. "Do you think my mommy was pretty?"

"She was beautiful, honey." His voice choked, and he swallowed. "Just like you are. In fact, your hair is the same color as hers. It makes me think of your mommy."

She gave him a solemn look—and he braced for more questions. But instead of continuing the conversation, she edged around him and walked toward the door. "Can I have my water?"

"Sure." He picked up the glass off the dresser and handed it to her.

She took a long drink, passed it back, and traipsed down the hall toward her room, trailing her blanket behind her.

Frowning, he followed her. He was missing something here—but for the life of him he couldn't figure out what it was.

"Would you like me to read you a story now?" He fiddled with the covers as she climbed into bed.

"No, thank you." She tucked the blanket under her chin and turned toward the wall.

He'd been dismissed.

After a few moments, Craig retreated to his own room, shoving his fingers through his hair as he crossed to the window. Ominous clouds had begun to mass at sunset, and now the moon and stars were hidden behind a black mantle.

The unsettled weather matched his mood.

But why was he so…uneasy? Vicki appeared to be calm. There'd been no tears. No tantrums. No displays of temper.

Yet he couldn't help feeling that somehow he'd just made a big mistake.

* * *

Unless she hurried, her plan to cut a wide swath around Craig since that post-spaghetti dinner kiss he'd dropped on her cheek three days ago could be in peril.

Craig's car wasn't in front of Edith's house as she swung onto Lighthouse Lane after the endless faculty meeting that had delayed her after school, but he could arrive any second.

She had to get Maddie ASAP and beat a fast retreat.

After parking her car, she hurried toward Edith's back door.

Unfortunately, Chester waylaid her in the yard. "Afternoon, Kate. Do you have a minute?"

Tamping down her impatience, she veered off the path toward the older man, who was at last putting the finishing touches on the guest cottage. "What's up, Chester?"

"Would you mind holding this door knocker in place while I screw it on? It'll only take a minute, and I could use another pair of hands. Edith's been too busy with the girls to help me out today."

"Sure."

The one minute stretched to five as Chester fiddled with the knocker and Kate fidgeted.

As soon as he pronounced the job done, she took off at a trot for the door. "Gotta run, Chester. It's coming along."

"Thanks." He waved and went back to work.

Edith opened the door as she approached. "I see Chester put you to work."

"Only for a couple of minutes. Sorry for the delay today."

"No problem." The other woman cocked her head. "Are you in a rush?"

Of course Edith had picked up on her agitation.

"Yes. I have a huge to-do list for tonight. Is Maddie ready?"

"The girls have been engrossed in a puzzle, and I didn't want to disturb them until you got here. Come on in and I'll get her jacket."

Kate followed her into the kitchen. In the adjacent sunroom,

Maddie and Vicki were kneeling on their chairs, elbows on the glass-topped wrought iron table, fitting puzzle pieces together.

"Here we go." Edith reentered the kitchen. "Maddie, your mommy's here."

Her daughter's lips drooped. "But we're almost done."

"You can finish it tomorrow, honey." Kate took the coat from Edith. "Mommy's got chores to do tonight."

Heaving a loud sigh, Maddie made a project out of climbing down off her chair, then trudged into the kitchen, dragging her feet. Molasses had nothing on her daughter.

Hard as Kate tried to appear calm and unruffled, not much got past Edith's eagle eye.

"You seem on edge."

"I'm fine. Come on, Maddie, we have to go."

Just as Maddie reached her, the doorbell rang.

Drat.

Edith brightened. "That must be Craig. I'll be back in a sec."

While her neighbor trotted toward the living room, Kate bundled Maddie into her coat, grabbed her hand, and towed her foot-dragging daughter toward the back door.

"Wait, Mommy." Maddie hung back. "Aren't we going to say hello to the lootenin?"

"Not today. I'm in a hurry."

As she gave Maddie's arm a gentle tug, a yelp came from the sunroom, followed by a clatter.

Double drat.

Much as she'd like to ignore that ominous noise, she wasn't wired that way.

"Wait here, honey." Leaving Maddie in the kitchen, she dashed toward the sunroom. Did a quick assessment from the threshold.

Vicki was on the floor, fat tears rolling down her cheeks, her chair overturned beside her. There wasn't any visible sign of damage.

Kate crossed to the girl, dropped to one knee, and smoothed back her hair. "What happened, sweetie?"

"The ch-chair tipped over when I t-tried to slide off."

"Does anything hurt?"

Vicki shook her head. "No, but it s-scared me."

She helped the girl up and gave her one more inspection. "It would scare me too. But you're fine now."

"What's the problem?"

Craig dropped down beside her, his faint, masculine after-shave invading her senses. And his blue eyes, mere inches away, sucked her in like a relentless tide—and left her floundering.

"The chair tipped. She's fine." Her explanation came out a tad breathless.

A tiny flame sparked to life in his baby blues. "Thanks for coming to the rescue."

"All in a day's work." She stood and eased away.

Thank goodness he stayed at Vicki's level, giving her a minute to rein in her pounding pulse.

"Are you sure you're not hurt, honey?" He reached out and tucked his daughter's hair behind her ear.

She sniffled again and nodded.

"We'll finish the puzzle tomorrow, Vicki." Maddie joined them and gave her friend's shoulder a consoling pat.

"Well. That's enough excitement for one day." Edith stepped forward and handed Vicki's jacket to Craig.

Hands clasped behind her, Maddie watched as he helped his

daughter slide her arms through the sleeves. "Are you going to kiss Mommy goodbye again?"

Heat surged up her neck and across her cheeks.

Could the floor please open up and swallow her now?

She risked a peek at Craig.

The flush on the back of his neck spoke volumes as he buttoned Vicki's jacket—but his response was measured. "That was a thank-you for such a delicious meal. What was your favorite part of the dinner, Vicki?"

"The chocolate cake."

Craig finished buttoning her coat and stood. "I agree. And Mrs. Shaw is a wonderful baker too. I'll bet you also had a treat today, didn't you?"

"Uh-huh. Oatmeal cookies."

"We helped her bake them," Maddie offered.

Craig's deft distraction had sidetracked the girls.

Hard to say how effective his deflection strategy had been with their shared babysitter, though.

"See you tomorrow, Edith." Craig took Vicki's hand. "Bye, Maddie. Take care, Kate."

Once again, a blush bloomed on her cheeks when their gazes connected.

As Edith ushered Craig and Vicki toward the front door, Maddie inspected her. "Why is your face red, Mommy?"

Further confirmation that the diplomacy gene was missing from the MacDonald women.

"I'm getting hot standing here in my coat. Let's go."

Any hope of escaping out the back door before Edith returned vanished, however, when the older woman hurried back into the room. She must have practically pushed the other duo out.

"So he kissed you, hmm?"

Play this cool, Kate—even if the blush that's the bane of red-heads is again rearing its ugly head.

"It was a peck on the cheek."

"Uh-huh."

"Edith." Kate tried for a stern tone. "Don't get ideas."

The woman smirked. "It would appear I'm not the only one with ideas."

Shaking her head, Kate strode toward the door. "You're hopeless."

"No." Edith followed her. "Hope*ful*."

"I give up."

"An excellent plan—because if you ask me, this one's a keeper."

"I'm out of here." Taking a firm grip on Maddie's hand, Kate led the little girl out the door and down the steps.

"Mommy." Maddie had to trot to keep up with her as she zipped across the grass, heading for the gate that separated the two yards. "What's a keeper?"

"It's something you always want to have with you."

A description that fit Craig Cole to a T—even if she wasn't yet ready to do anything about it.

* * *

"Sorry to interrupt, sir. But I thought you'd want to take this call."

As his executive petty officer spoke from the threshold of his office, Craig set aside the material he was reviewing to prep for the role he'd inherited on the Nantucket Shipwreck & Lifesaving Museum board.

"Who is it?"

"Katherine MacDonald. She said it's important."

It must be, if she was calling him after that embarrassing fiasco at Edith's yesterday. From the quick glance he'd aimed her direction as he and Vicki left, he'd gotten the distinct impression she hoped their paths wouldn't cross again until the next millennium.

"Go ahead and put her through."

As Barlow exited, Craig ignored the man's knowing grin. He had more important things to think about than his aide's slight impertinence.

Like an appealing charter captain with flashing green eyes and hair the color of glowing embers.

The phone rang, and he picked it up. Greeted Kate.

"I'm sorry to bother you at work."

At the distress in her voice, he sat up straighter, nerves tingling as they had in his rescue-swimmer days after he'd been assigned a dangerous mission. "No problem. What's up?"

"Edith had to run to church to deal with a Daffodil Festival-related catastrophe, and since I'm not subbing today she asked if I could bring Maddie over this afternoon and watch Vicki while she was gone. I'm at her house now. But a situation has come up that I think you may want to deal with."

"Is Vicki hurt?" He tightened his grip on the phone.

"No. Nothing like that." Her volume dropped. "I was working on a manuscript and I thought the girls were doing another puzzle in the sunroom. But they got too quiet, and when I went to check on them I discovered they'd rounded up a pair of scissors and cut Vicki's hair. They were trying to color what was left with markers. I can't get any explanation out of either of them. But it's…a mess."

"I can be there in less than ten minutes. Hang tight."

The instant the call ended, Craig stuffed the Lifesaving

Museum material into his briefcase, told Barlow he was leaving for the day, and drove to Edith's house as fast as the bone-jarring cobblestones would allow.

As Kate had warned him, Vicki was a wreck. The two little girls were huddled together on one chair in Edith's sunroom, their hands stained with black streaks. They hung their heads when he appeared, giving him an excellent view of the chop job they'd done on Vicki's hair. Tufts of varying lengths stuck out in all directions, and they'd tried to color what remained with a black marker.

In light of her bewildered shrug, Kate was as confused as he was.

One thing for certain, though—neither girl was prone to mischief. They had a motive that was logical to them…if he could ferret it out.

And if he did get an explanation, his gut told him that the way he handled the situation was going to have a huge impact on his relationship with his daughter.

Praying he'd say and do the right things, Craig crossed the room and dropped to the balls of his feet in front of the two girls. Kate hovered in the background but stayed close—thank goodness. If he got into trouble, at least there was an experienced reinforcement on hand.

"Hey." He kept his tone gentle and reached for their small hands. "We're going to fix this."

Maddie peeked up at him first. "Are you mad?"

"Were you being naughty?"

"No. We were trying to make everything better."

The incomprehensible explanation seemed to make sense to the two girls.

"It wasn't Maddie's fault." Vicki raised her quivering chin.

"She only cut the back. I asked her to because I couldn't reach it."

"Was this your idea?"

His daughter nodded.

"Maddie, let's go wash your hands." Kate moved into the room, waiting as Maddie slid off the chair before directing her next comment to Craig. "We'll be down the hall if you need us."

He mouthed a silent *thank-you*.

As mother and daughter disappeared, Vicki's chin continued to wobble, her face a study in misery.

The knot in Craig's stomach tightened.

Now what?

Pick her up. Hold her.

Without questioning the source of that advice, he lifted Vicki off the chair and folded her tiny frame in his arms, tucking her head against his shoulder as he stood.

When had he last held her like this?

Too long ago to remember.

But it felt good. And right.

"Hey." He stroked what was left of her hair. "You don't have to be upset. I know you had a reason for doing this. If we sit together in that big chair in Mrs. Shaw's living room, will you tell me about it?"

A sniffle was her only response.

Choosing to interpret that as a yes, he walked into the next room and eased into the wing chair, nestling her into the crook of his arm as he settled her on his lap.

They remained like that for a full minute, but when the silence lengthened, Craig took the initiative. "Didn't you like your long hair anymore, honey?"

She shook her head, leaving it burrowed in his chest.

141

He fingered the short, stubby locks, a pang echoing in his heart. "You had such pretty hair. Just like your mommy's."

"I don't want to be like Mommy."

He did a double take at her fierceness. "Why not?"

"Because when you look at her picture you're sad. I don't want you to be sad when you look at me. I thought if I changed my hair, you might be h-happier when you're with m-me."

He bit back a word he never used. Clenched his teeth.

The haircutting escapade was a cry for love. For attention. For affection. For joy.

Man, had he blown it big-time with his daughter.

But giving up wasn't an option. He'd fix this.

Somehow.

Craig smoothed the hair back from his daughter's forehead. "I'm not sad when I look at you, Vicki. Because I love what's in here"—he touched her chest, above her heart—"more than what's up here." He stroked her hair again. "I love you for who you are. Sometimes people look the same, like you and your mommy, but every single person in the whole world is different. There's nobody else just like you, and there never will be. You're special. And I love you for that—no matter what color your hair is."

"But I make you sad."

"No, you don't." Not anymore. Not ever again. "When your mommy and brother went to heaven, I was so sad I forgot about everything else. I'm sorry about that now. I wish I could start over with you from the very beginning. But I promise, from now on I'm not going to think about yesterday anymore. I'm going to think about tomorrow, and all the fun we're going to have together."

She studied him, with eyes that from this day forward he

would think of as Vicki's, not Nicole's. "Promise?"

"Promise. In fact, let's start the fun tonight by having chocolate chip waffles for dinner."

Her face lit up. "I've never had those."

"Me, neither. But we'll figure out how to make them together." Surely there were recipes for such a dish on the Net.

Holding Vicki close, he rose, turned—and found Kate watching him, the tenderness in her unguarded expression disrupting the steady rhythm of his pulse.

She blinked and angled away. "Um...Maddie and I are heading home."

"We are too." He waved a hand over Vicki's hair. "Any suggestions on how to remedy this?"

"My hairdresser may be able to salvage it—and she works late on Thursdays. I could call her and see if she can squeeze in an emergency."

"I'd appreciate it."

"Give me a minute."

As she disappeared into Edith's kitchen, Maddie edged closer to them. "Mommy says we can make daffy hats tomorrow, Vicki."

His daughter didn't loosen her grip around his neck as she responded—which was fine with him. "That will be fun."

"What's a daffy hat?" Craig adjusted her weight against his hip.

"It's a hat decorated with daffodils," Maddie told him. "For the festival on Saturday. You're going, aren't you?"

Vicki edged back so she could see his face. "We are, aren't we, Daddy?"

The town was buzzing with festival preparations, but other than hanging a daffodil wreath on tiny Brant Point Light, the

Coast Guard had no official involvement. And he'd been too busy to make any personal plans for the event.

"I guess we can. I'll have to find out more about it."

"The Daffodil Festival is always fun." Maddie swung around as Kate reentered. "Isn't it, Mommy?"

"Yes. A highlight of the year." She crossed the room and handed him a slip of paper. "I jotted down the address. Just ask for Chloe when you get there. She'll be expecting you."

"Can Vicki and the lootenin go to the parade with us, Mommy? I told him we were making hats tomorrow."

"Were you planning to go?" Kate directed the question to him as she adjusted Maddie's collar.

"I didn't have plans one way or the other. What's the story on the hats?"

"A lot of people decorate hats to wear for the Daffy Hat Pageant. Mostly tourists, to be honest. But I thought the girls would get a kick out of it." She tucked a springy lock of hair behind her ear. "If the weather's decent, Maddie and I are going to watch the antique car parade on Main Street. You're welcome to join us, if you like."

Huh.

Their impromptu kiss must not have sent her running in the opposite direction, as he'd expected.

Or was empathy for Vicki the motive behind the invitation? Who knew?

But if he wanted to stick by his vow to remain unattached, accepting would *not* be a smart idea.

As he opened his mouth to decline, Vicki spoke.

"Could we, Daddy? Please? It would be fun."

One glance at those hopeful blue-green eyes inches from his—plus her shorn hair—and he was sunk.

"I guess we can. Tell me where and when to meet."

Kate filled him in on the details, and five minutes later he and Vicki were on their way to see Chloe.

But as they drove through the narrow streets, a rush of second thoughts swept over him. Attending the festival in the company of the appealing charter captain and her charming daughter wasn't going to do a thing to neutralize the chemistry between them. Just the opposite.

Yet for once he didn't feel a rush of panic at that thought. Perhaps because he was beginning to accept that God had forgiven him for whatever role he'd played in the tragedy that had taken his family. While he wasn't ready to be that generous with himself, he was getting close to finding the strength to let go of the guilt and move on.

However…Kate's connection to the sea—and the risk that carried—remained a major stumbling block.

One he hadn't a clue how to overcome.

12

"There he is, Mommy!"

At Maddie's excited comment, Kate followed the direction of her daughter's finger.

In seconds she spotted Craig on the other side of the street, wearing khaki slacks and a chest-hugging golf shirt that showcased notable biceps. Vicki was hidden by the legs of spectators lined up on Main Street for the parade, but she caught a quick glimpse of blond hair. Excellent. Chloe had at least managed to get rid of the dye from the marker.

"Mommy, aren't you going to wave at him?" Maddie tugged on her hand.

"Yes, honey. I was waiting until he turned toward us."

A partial truth, at best. She was also waiting for her pulse to settle down after the leap it had taken the instant she'd spotted him. Except the parade would be over before that happened.

He caught sight of her then, and taking advantage of a balky engine that left a temporary gap in the lineup of vintage vehicles, he swept Vicki into his arms, strode across the cobblestone street, and stepped onto the sidewalk.

"Those are amazing hats, ladies."

"We put the daffodils on them this morning." Maddie touched the straw brim of her ribbon-and-flower-bedecked bonnet. "We found pink ones for yours, Vicki. Show her, Mommy."

Kate knelt in front of Vicki. Chloe had done a superb job of salvaging the child's locks, giving her a wispy pixie cut that flattered her delicate, heart-shaped face. "Pink daffodils are rare and special, but we found a few for your hat because you're a special girl. Do you like it?"

Beaming, Vicki examined the straw creation, gently touching the fragile cups of the flowers. "I love it. Thank you."

"You're very welcome. Let's try it on."

Once Kate settled it on her head, she secured it with a bow under Vicki's chin. "There. The two prettiest hats for the two prettiest girls on Nantucket."

As she started to rise, a hand under her elbow steadied her.

"Thank you for doing that." The appealing dimple in Craig's cheek did nothing to steady her erratic pulse.

"It was no big deal."

"It was for Vicki."

"Kids are easy to please."

"Only if you have the knack."

"You do."

He exhaled and shook his head. "Not in light of what happened Thursday."

"That's not true." Kate lowered her voice. "I got the story from…" She pointed down to her daughter, who was engaged in an animated conversation with Vicki as they watched the cars go by. "And I caught the end of your conversation with…" She motioned toward Vicki. "You handled it well."

"I wouldn't have had to handle it at all if I'd been the kind of father I should have been from the beginning."

"What matters now is what you do going forward. And from what I can see, you're on the right track."

"I hope so." He reached into his pocket and withdrew his phone. "Would you mind taking a picture of me and Vicki?"

"I'd be happy to." She reached for the cell, trying not to let the brush of his long, lean fingers distract her. "Say cheese." As they complied, she pressed the button to capture the image of the smiling, blue-eyed man and winsome blond-haired girl for posterity, praying it would be the first of many to come as they began a new chapter in their lives.

And despite the fear that held her back from pursuing a romance with the beguiling Coast Guard commander, she couldn't help but wish that a few of those pictures would include her and Maddie.

No matter how unwise that was.

* * *

As Kate handed him the phone and he tucked it back in his pocket, Craig wasn't quite certain how to interpret the sudden wistfulness in her expression.

But she didn't give him an opportunity to dwell on that puzzle, calling his attention to the girls instead.

"I can't believe how quickly Maddie and Vicki became fast friends, can you?"

"It doesn't take long when people click."

Kate's heightened color suggested she'd interpreted his comment more broadly than he'd intended—but that was okay. The statement was true for all relationships.

Including theirs.

As the vintage cars continued to clatter past on the cobblestone street, Craig stole surreptitious glances at his date for the day.

Date.

That was too generous a term.

But with all the electricity flying between them, they could be headed toward that path.

Strange how life worked.

He'd come to Nantucket to reconnect with the sea and his daughter. Romance hadn't even been on his radar.

Yet the woman beside him was making him rethink his vow to live out his life without a partner.

As the parade wound down, Kate motioned toward the sky, where dark clouds were massing in the distance. "Those don't bode well for the tailgate picnic in 'Sconset."

"Were you planning to go?"

"No. This is enough activity for one day." Kate reached for her daughter's hand. "Let's go home, honey. I think it's going to rain."

"I'd offer you a ride, but we're parked at the station. It will probably be shorter for you to walk home."

"That's true." Kate took a step back as the crowd around them dispersed. "See you at church tomorrow."

"We'll be there. Thanks for inviting us today. The girls enjoyed it—and I did too." Without debating the pros and cons, he took a step closer, laid a hand on her shoulder, and brushed his lips across her cheek.

Her breath caught, but before she could respond Maddie spoke. "How come you kissed Mommy again, Lootenin?"

"To say thank you for the hat she decorated for Vicki." He didn't break eye contact as he spoke—nor did he remove his hand from her shoulder. "And because I like her."

"She likes you too. Don't you, Mommy?"

A blush bloomed on Kate's cheeks and she edged away, forcing him to release his hold. "I, uh, had your sweater cleaned. I'll bring it to church for you tomorrow." She tugged on her daughter's hand. "Come on, Maddie. We don't want to get caught in the rain. Bye, Vicki. Craig." With that, she towed Maddie down the sidewalk.

"What are you going to do with the picture you asked Mrs. MacDonald to take of us?"

At Vicki's question, Craig pulled his attention away from Kate and refocused on his daughter. "I'll show you as soon as we get home."

Twenty minutes later, after downloading the photo to his computer, he printed a copy and held it out for Vicki to see. "What do you think?"

"I like it."

"And now comes the best part." Craig rose from the desk in his spare bedroom and retrieved a bag from the top of a filing cabinet. After opening it, he withdrew a small brass frame and slid the photo inside. Then, leading the way, he placed it front and center on his dresser, moving the other picture to the side.

His daughter clapped her hands in delight—meaning that, for once, he hadn't blown the fatherhood role.

"It's perfect there, Daddy."

"I agree. But you know what's even more perfect?"

"What?"

"This." He swooped down, scooped her up, and twirled her around, cradling her in his arms as she shrieked and giggled.

When he stopped, she threw her arms around his neck. "I love you, Daddy."

"I love you too."

And as he held her close, he gave thanks for the four sweetest words he'd heard in years.

Maybe there were still storms ahead, but at least he was on course toward his destination.

* * *

At the ring of her phone on Sunday night, Kate set aside the manuscript she was editing at the dining room table. The timing of the call was spot-on. She could use a break. Besides, it wasn't as if she'd made much progress since putting Maddie to bed. It was hard to edit when exhaustion was blurring the words on the page.

She picked up her cell, stifled a yawn, and said hello without bothering to check caller ID.

"Kate, it's Craig. Edith told me at church that you stayed home because Maddie had an asthma attack last night. I thought I'd call and see how she was doing."

Her sleepiness vanished as the mellow baritone voice came over the line, and she rose and wandered toward the living room. "I appreciate that. It was a bad one. And she had another episode this morning. All in all, it's been a tough day. She's already in bed." She smothered another yawn with her hand.

"It sounds like you should be too."

"I wish." She sank onto the couch. "But I have a manuscript due next Friday, and I'm subbing the first three days of the week. I need to put in another hour or two on it tonight."

"I won't keep you, then. But I did have one other reason for calling. If the weather cooperates next Sunday, I thought I'd take Vicki on a picnic to one of the beaches outside town. She hasn't wiggled her toes in the sand yet. I was hoping you could give me a recommendation."

"Dionis is lovely—and it won't be too crowded yet."

"Got it. On to part two of my question. Would you and Maddie like to join us?"

Her heart stuttered as she locked onto Mac's painting over the mantel and tried to collect her thoughts. "The girls would enjoy that."

"No question about it—and I would too."

That was direct.

Just like the remark he'd made yesterday as they'd parted after the parade. The one that had kept her awake last night during the few peaceful stretches while Maddie had slept and she could have clocked a bit of much-needed shut-eye. The one that was playing havoc with her peace of mind. The one he'd made right after he kissed her.

For the second time.

As the clock on the mantel ticked, she tried to be rational. Prudent. Cautious.

Yet her heart kept getting in the way, urging her to accept.

"Kate, it's a picnic—with children in tow." Craig's quiet, steady reassurance came over the line. "If it's any consolation, though, I'm nervous about this too. I never intended to get involved with anyone again—but I can't ignore the chemistry between us. I've come to believe the Lord led me to Nantucket— and to you—for a purpose. While I realize the hurdles we face may be bigger than we can overcome, I'd like to test the waters, see where this relationship could lead."

Also direct.

And she couldn't dispute anything Craig had said. There *was* chemistry between them. And like Craig, she couldn't write off their meeting—or remarks like the one she'd overheard him making to Vicki about chocolate chip waffles—to mere coincidence.

She rose and moved closer to Mac's landscape. Ran a gentle finger over the paint he'd laid down with such care to create the scene of timeless beauty. Leaned closer as a tiny whimsical touch she'd never noticed during the six years the painting had graced her mantel suddenly jumped out at her.

Tucked into one corner, a tiny mouse was peeking out of its hole, preparing to enter the larger world despite the hazards that might lurk nearby.

Maybe she ought to follow its example. Go for it, as Mac would have said.

Her fingers still resting on the canvas, Kate took the leap. "I accept."

A few seconds of silence ticked by.

"You mean...you'll go?" Craig sounded stunned.

"Do you want to retract the invitation?"

"No." His response was immediate—and definite. "I just didn't expect you to agree so fast."

"I'm not certain I should have—but I can't ignore the chemistry, either. I have a host of fears to get past before this could ever work, though."

"I do too. I lost one family to the sea. I have to admit I'm a bit wary about getting involved with a woman who spends most of her days on the water. But I'm beginning to accept that what happened to Nicole and Aaron was a tragic fluke. A bad combination of circumstances that would never happen again. I'm not there yet, though. So we both have issues to work through. We'll just have to proceed with caution. Fair enough?"

"Yes. And speaking of caution...why don't Maddie and I meet you at the beach?"

"Whatever makes you most comfortable is fine with me. About one o'clock?"

"We'll be there."

"In the meantime, get some sleep."

Not likely, given this latest adrenaline-pumping development.

But she had work to do anyway.

Yet when she returned to her editing task, her concentration remained off.

Except this time, fatigue wasn't the culprit.

13

How could it be Sunday already?

Kate rolled onto her back and pried open her eyelids. Stared at the white ceiling in her bedroom. Where had the week gone? It was a blur of subbing, finishing the manuscript, seeing to the repair of the *Lucy Sue*'s propeller, and dealing with another asthma attack.

Thankfully, her supply of adrenaline hadn't run out.

Yawning, she swung her legs to the floor. At least she'd been too busy to think about Craig—although she *had* finally managed to return his sweater via Edith.

But she'd be seeing him today.

Her stomach fluttered.

Maybe she should cancel the picnic.

But Maddie—and Vicki—would be disappointed. Chickening out wouldn't be fair to them.

Huffing out a breath, she retrieved a towel from the linen closet and headed for the shower. She was getting all worked up over nothing. If the atmosphere got too uncomfortable during today's outing, the solution was simple and straightforward.

Don't repeat it.

Except nothing about being around Craig was simple or straightforward—a truth reinforced when she and Maddie arrived at church and found him and Vicki sitting behind Edith and

Chester. In the spot she and Maddie usually occupied.

Keeping a firm grip on Maddie's hand, she steered her daughter toward a pew on the other side.

"Why can't we sit by Vicki?" Maddie's query carried throughout the church, and the foursome on the other side turned in unison.

Pasting on a smile, Kate waved at the other group and bent down to whisper to Maddie. "Because I don't want you and Vicki talking during the service. We'll see them afterward."

Though her daughter pouted, at least she didn't put up a fuss.

The service was uneventful—except for the few surreptitious glances she sent toward Craig that ratcheted up her pulse.

Not a comforting omen for the picnic to come.

As the last hymn wound down, she took Maddie's hand and exited. Like the first Sunday Craig had shown up at church, she was tempted to flee. But running from her feelings wasn't going to change them. Craig had had the courage to address his head-on, and she should follow his example. So today she stood her ground.

When Craig stepped out the door a couple of minutes later, followed by Edith and Chester, he released Vicki's hand and the little girl ran toward Maddie. The two youngsters launched into an enthusiastic exchange while Kate waited for the adults to catch up.

Edith beamed at her as they drew close. "You have a beautiful day for a picnic on the beach."

If she'd had her druthers, Kate wouldn't have told the Lighthouse Lane matchmaker about the outing—but the girls had been jabbering about it all week. No way could she have kept it a secret. Nevertheless, she'd done her best to downplay the excursion.

Edith, however, hadn't bought that. The twinkle in her eye was more pronounced than ever.

"We're still on, aren't we?" Craig waved at a honeybee that had taken a liking to him.

"Yes. I should have called this week to see if I could bring anything, but my schedule was crazy. It's not too late, though. Would you like me to pick up a contribution at the store before we join you?"

"No, thanks. I've got it covered."

"We'll see you at one, then." She took Maddie's hand. "Come on, honey. We have to go home and change our clothes."

"Wear those cute white shorts with the green top." Edith grinned at her.

Kate shot the woman a silent back-off warning. The shorts were a tad too snug and the boat-neck top dipped too low for her comfort level. That's why she rarely wore the outfit—as Edith well knew.

"I haven't decided what to wear yet." She directed her next comment to Craig. "See you soon." Taking a firmer grip on Maddie's hand, she led her daughter toward their car and buckled her in.

Once in the driver's seat, she aimed the car toward home, following the familiar route. In control behind the wheel and clear about her destination.

Which was *not* a metaphor for her life these days.

Unfortunately.

* * *

"When is Maddie going to get here?"

At Vicki's question, Craig finished spreading a large blanket on the beach. "In a few minutes, honey. We're a little early."

She hovered close, watching the breakers. "Is the water going to come up here?"

"No." He sat on the blanket, took off his deck shoes, and rolled his jeans up. The waves could be a tad intimidating for a child who'd never been on a beach—which was why he'd arrived early. "It creeps up slowly, and then creeps back out again. See that line of shells?" He pointed out the high water mark, denoted by various bits of flotsam. "That's as far as it comes, unless there's a bad storm. And today is sunny. See how blue the sky is?"

She surveyed the cloudless expanse above her—but showed no interest in approaching the water.

Craig unbuckled her sandals, stood, and took her hand. "Let's see if we can find any shells."

He led her to the high water mark, then gradually closer to the water, until a larger wave sent an arc of water high enough to tickle their toes. Vicki squealed and scampered back, tugging on his hand.

Instead of moving, Craig leaned down and drew a smiley face in the wet sand with his finger. "This is even better than crayons." Edging toward the water as Vicki clung to his hand, he drew the sun. "What would you like to draw?"

She eased closer to examine his handiwork. "A flower."

"Have at it."

Keeping tabs on the waves, she drew a facsimile of a daisy.

"I like that." Craig gave it his full attention. "It reminds me of—"

"Vicki!"

At Maddie's shout, his daughter straightened up and took off

158

at a run for the approaching duo.

Craig followed more slowly. Maddie, already barefoot, was dressed in shorts and a T-shirt, like his daughter. But it was Kate who drew—and held—his attention.

She'd exchanged her church clothes for cropped beige pants and a green-and-beige striped knit top that showed off her slender figure. Although she'd restrained her hair at her nape with a barrette, a few springy curls had escaped to frame her face. Her sunglasses hid her glorious eyes, but she could do nothing to disguise the appealing curve of her lips.

As he drew close, Maddie grinned and waved. "Hi, Lootenin."

"Hello, Maddie."

Showing no compunction about getting close to the water, she scampered straight toward the breakers, splashing through the waves as they washed over her feet.

Emboldened by her friend's confidence, Vicki fell in behind her.

"Don't get too wet, Maddie." Kate cupped her hands around her mouth as she called out.

Busy dodging waves, the youngster didn't acknowledge the directive.

"I have a feeling the change of clothes I brought will come in handy." Kate shook her head and set down the kid-size pails and shovels she'd been lugging. Shrugging the large beach bag from her shoulder, she let it drop to the sand beside the blanket he'd spread.

"I should have brought an extra set of clothes too." More proof his parenting skills were lacking.

Kate dismissed his concern with a wave. "Vicki will be fine.

I'm overprotective about Maddie because of the asthma." Kicking off her flip-flops, she sat on the blanket and motioned toward the large brown bag and small cooler on one edge. "What's for lunch?"

He dropped down beside her. "I went to Something Natural and got sandwiches and cookies. I hope that's not too simple."

"Not at all." Her features softened as she gave the sandy stretch a sweep. "Mac and I used to pick up sandwiches and escape to the beach on a regular basis."

"Tell me more about him." Talking about Kate's husband hadn't been his top priority today, but it wouldn't hurt to learn more about what he was up against.

She scooped up a handful of sand. Let it drift through her fingers. "Every day with Mac was an adventure. And special days were amazing. One year on my birthday he enlisted Edith's help and scoured the local gardens to fill the house with flowers so we could have a picnic in a garden despite the rain."

"Impressive." And not something he'd ever have thought to do.

"It was vintage Mac. But my favorite birthday was the year he set up a formal dinner on the beach at Great Point, complete with white linen tablecloth, china, and silver. He even rented a tux, and we danced barefoot in the sand while some of his musician friends entertained us."

"Wow." The man had him beat hands down in the romance department. "That's a hard act to follow."

Kate took off her sunglasses and locked onto his gaze. "Everyone has their own gifts to offer and is special in their own way. Just like you told Vicki."

Warmth radiated through him. "Thanks."

"Mommy, I'm hungry. Can we eat?"

The girls ran up, their feet spraying sand in all directions. Kate brushed the grains off the blanket as he reached for the bag.

"Lunch is served...unless there are any objections?"

Vicki plopped down beside him. "I'm hungry too."

He glanced at Kate.

"Count me in."

As Craig unpacked the food and Kate distributed it, the girls chattered, putting a damper on adult conversation. But after the lively meal was over, they scampered off with buckets and pails to build a sand castle while Craig stowed the leftovers.

"I think I've discovered the nation's untapped energy source." He closed the cooler and stretched his legs out in front of him, crossed them at the ankles, and leaned back on his palms.

Kate's mouth quirked as she stifled a yawn. "The Energizer Bunny has nothing on kids, that's for sure. I wish I could tap into it."

He examined the faint shadows under her lashes, the pinch of weariness at the corners of her mouth. "You look tired."

"Busy week."

"Why don't you stretch out and rest for a few minutes? I'll watch the girls."

She caught her lower lip between her teeth. "That wouldn't be polite."

"You don't have to dazzle me with your sparkling wit or keep me entertained every minute, Kate. I'm content just to share the afternoon with you."

"If you're sure you don't mind...it would be bliss to drift for a few minutes."

"I don't mind in the least."

After a nanosecond pause, Kate pulled a rolled-up beach towel from her bag, stretched out, and positioned it under her head. "Give me ten."

"Take as long as you like. I'll enjoy the scenery."

Within five minutes, her even breathing suggested she'd fallen into a sound sleep—giving him an opportunity to take in the view.

Of her.

He traced the graceful curve of her cheek, studied the dusting of freckles on her nose. In slumber, she appeared younger. More vulnerable. Sleep had wiped the tension from her features, erased the faint furrows of worry that often marred her brow. A slight breeze played with the unruly curls around her face that seemed oh-so-soft.

Dare he touch one to find out?

No.

Not while she was asleep.

But before this day ended, he intended to satisfy his curiosity.

* * *

A child's shriek tugged Kate back from the depths of oblivion. Maddie!

Struggling to rouse herself, she tried to sit up. But a gentle, firm hand pressed her back.

"Relax, Kate. She's fine. They're trying to catch a seagull." Craig's voice.

She tried to shake off the last vestiges of sleep. Orient herself.

They were...on a picnic. On the beach. Craig was watching

the girls while she took a quick rest.

Except she had a feeling it hadn't been quick.

"How long did I sleep?"

"Forty-five minutes."

"What?" She pushed herself upright. "I'm so sorry."

"Don't be. I wasn't bored."

His tone was difficult to interpret.

She shoved a few loose tendrils of hair back from her face and went with a safe response. "Kids are more entertaining than watching TV."

"Yes—but they weren't the only ones I was watching." He took off his sunglasses to reveal eyes that had darkened in color and grown as restless as the sea before a storm. "You're beautiful when you sleep."

Her heart slammed against her rib cage. "Not so much when I'm awake, huh?" Hard as she tried, she couldn't quite pull off a teasing tone.

"Awake moves you from beautiful to stunning." When he reached over and captured one of her curls, her breath hitched. "Just as soft as I expected."

As he worked the strands between his fingertips. Kate cast a quick glance at the girls, who were engrossed in digging a moat around their castle.

"They've seen me kiss you before, Kate."

Her gaze jerked back to his, an arc of electricity leaping between them as he signaled his intent.

And this wasn't going to be a casual peck on the cheek.

But he was warning her. Giving her an opening to back off. Leaving the decision up to her.

What should she do?

She'd accepted this invitation with full knowledge it would

move their relationship to a new level—and she'd thought she was ready for that.

But was she?

Craig angled toward her and enfolded her hand in his. "If it's any consolation, Kate, I'm as nervous about this as you are. I haven't been on a date in years."

As she examined his strong, lean fingers, she drew a quivering breath.

Not since Mac died had she felt so safe. Secure. Protected. Cared for. Wanted.

And Craig's candid admission did more to quell the butterflies in her stomach than anything else he could have said or done. "I don't want to rush."

"Me, neither. But I think we're past the kiss-on-the-cheek stage, don't you?"

At the hint of humor in his eyes, her comfort level edged up another notch. "I guess so. But I...I'm sort of out of practice."

"That makes two of us. What do you say we brush up on our skills?"

Without waiting for her to respond, he erased the distance between them. Cupping the back of her head with his hand, he captured her lips in a kiss as gentle as a balmy Nantucket summer breeze.

When he at last backed off a few inches, his breath was a puff of warmth against her cheek. "Not bad, considering we're both rusty."

It took her a moment to find her voice. "Yeah."

"And it will only improve with practice."

His comment did nothing to slow her racing pulse.

A sudden gust of wind whipped past, stirring the sand around them, and Craig scanned the sky. "We timed this outing well.

Mother Nature is being fickle."

Weather.

He was talking about the weather.

Forcing herself to switch gears, she surveyed the dark clouds gathering on the horizon—although the tempest that was brewing in the sky wouldn't hold a candle to the one raging in her heart.

She angled toward the surf line. "Maddie! Vicki! We have to leave. It's going to rain."

As she slipped on her flip-flops, Craig gathered up the remnants of their picnic and rose to fold up the blanket. While the girls trotted over, Kate collected their buckets and shovels.

"Before we go, may I take a picture of you three ladies over by the water?" Craig pulled out his phone.

"Yes!" Vicki took Maddie's hand and tugged her closer to the breakers.

Kate held back. "Why don't you just take a shot of the girls? They'd treasure it for—"

"Would you folks like me to take a picture of all of you together?"

An older man and his wife, beach chairs and towels in hand, stopped beside them on their trek to the parking lot from farther down the beach.

Craig took her hand. "I like that idea."

A family shot—like the one she'd found herself wishing for at the Daffodil Festival.

Yet she hesitated.

They weren't a family, and—

"Come on, Mommy!" Maddie called. "We can all squeeze together."

"Yeah." Craig grinned and gave her another tug. "I'm a good

squeezer."

It was impossible to resist the entreaties of the trio in their pseudo-family group.

Kate let him lead her over to the girls.

As they took up a position behind their daughters, Craig placed one hand on Vicki's shoulder and draped his arm around Kate.

"Say 'cheese!'" The older man positioned the cell.

After they complied, he examined his handiwork on the screen. "Nice family." He handed the phone back to Craig. "You folks enjoy the rest of your day." With a wave, he and his wife continued down the beach toward the sandy path that led to the parking lot.

While Kate slung the beach bag over her shoulder and nested the buckets, Craig tucked the phone in his pocket and retrieved the cooler and blanket. As they began their trek toward their cars, he once more claimed her hand, entwining his fingers with hers.

It was slow going through the deep, loose sand, and more than once Kate felt off balance.

But while she tried to blame her unsteadiness on the terrain, that was a lie. It had nothing to do with the shifting grains beneath her feet...and everything to do with the shifting landscape of her world.

* * *

"I like that picture, Daddy." Vicki watched, four hours later, as the shot of the four of them on the beach emerged from Craig's printer.

So did he. They looked like the family the man who'd taken their picture had assumed they were. The little girls—one fair, one dark—were holding hands. His arm was around Kate's shoulders, and she was leaning into him. They all seemed happy—and as if they belonged together.

"Where are we going to put it, Daddy?"

"We'll have to start a photo album. I'll get one this week."

"But can't we put this one where we can see it every day?"

"I like that idea. I think I have an extra frame in my bedroom."

"Let's go get it!"

Vicki led the way, and Craig opened his closet. Near as he could recall, there was an empty four-by-six frame in one of the boxes he hadn't gotten around to unpacking.

After pulling out the carton, he lifted the lid and dug through it until his fingers closed over the edge of the frame. But when he withdrew it, the glass was cracked and one corner of the wood had been crushed. A casualty of the move, most likely.

"It's broken." Vicki's mouth turned down.

He set the damaged frame aside, preparing to console her with a promise that he'd pick up a new one tomorrow, when the family shot on his dresser registered.

He froze.

No!

Fighting down a wave of panic, he tried to quash the idea that sprang to mind. It was too…final. Letting go was too hard.

Yet how could he move forward if he continued to cling to the past?

"Daddy?"

At Vicki's uncertain question, he tried to summon up a reassuring smile. "We'll get a new frame tomorrow. How does that sound?"

Instead of responding, she glanced at the photo on his

dresser. "You looked sad. Were you thinking about Mommy and Aaron?"

His daughter was way too intuitive.

But he wasn't going to lie to her.

"For a minute. This is a pretty picture, isn't it?" He rested his unsteady hand on top of the frame.

She regarded it in silence. "Yes. But it makes you sad. I think you should put up pictures that make you happy. Like that one." She pointed to the shot in his other hand.

Out of the mouths of babes…

Craig took a slow, deep breath.

Continuing to mourn for the past would do nothing except deprive him of a future. While Nicole and Aaron would always have a special place in his heart, the time had come to set his old memories aside and move on. To open himself to the opportunities the Lord had sent his way to create new memories…with a new family.

Fingers trembling, Craig reached for the koa-wood frame and slid the backing off. Removed the photo and replaced it with the one taken today, tucking the older one behind it. Set it on his dresser, beside the one of him and Vicki at the Daffodil Festival parade.

A small hand crept into his. "It's okay, Daddy. You have me."

Vision misting, he dropped to one knee beside the daughter he'd neglected for too long and pulled her close, sending a silent prayer of thanks heavenward for the blessing of her sweet, innocent love.

And for guidance as he entered the uncharted waters ahead.

14

Talk about an easy way to make a buck.

One hand on the wheel, Kate guided the *Lucy Sue* through the sea off Great Point and watched the three college-age anglers in the stern, who were doing more laughing than trolling. Just as well. Other than a few premature arrivals, the bluefish were still miles south of Nantucket on their trek north for the summer. There was little likelihood the lackadaisical fishermen would snag even one.

Not that they seemed to care. When they'd approached her on the dock, they'd assured her they were more interested in fresh air and sea breezes than catching fish. And after they'd flashed all those fifty-dollar bills at her, offering to pay more than her usual fee, why try to dissuade them? Her cash reserve could use a little extra padding after the expense of fixing her dinged propeller. If they had more money than sense, that was their problem.

Best of all, she hadn't even needed to call on Chester to assist as mate today, like she did with larger groups. Three people were a piece of cake—especially when they weren't all that serious about fishing and it was only a two-hour charter.

She made a wide arc to starboard on this glorious, sunny Friday that was ideal for cruising, if not for fishing. And unlike most trips, she wasn't too busy to enjoy it—and let herself daydream about an appealing Coast Guard commander who'd begun to play a large role in her life since last Sunday's beach picnic.

Her lips bowed.

He'd been stopping in every day after picking Vicki up, sometimes only long enough to claim a quick kiss, other days staying for an impromptu pizza or spaghetti dinner. Those family-type get-togethers were supplemented with phone calls that sometimes lasted far too late into the night. Although her sleep was suffering, she felt invigorated rather than tired.

That's what falling in love could do to you.

And she was falling. Hard. No question about it.

All at once, the brilliant sunlight dimmed, cooling the air, and she scanned the sky. A few clouds were scuttling across the blue expanse while their grayer cousins gathered on the horizon.

It seemed Nantucket's notoriously capricious weather was about to change.

But they should be fine for a while. Luckily they were more than halfway through this excursion.

Kate refocused on her passengers.

The three of them were lounging in the deck chairs, feet propped up, slugging back the bottles of water they'd brought on board and sharing rowdy laughs. They still held their fishing lines, but it was apparent their attention was elsewhere.

Turning away from the trio, Kate swung the *Lucy Sue* to port, keeping tabs on the sky and the sea. No sense venturing any farther out with—

At the sudden sound of a reel spinning out of control, Kate swung around.

One of the college guys vaulted to a standing position, his feet hitting the deck with a thump. "Hey! I've got a fish!"

As Kate put the engine in neutral and prepared to talk the lucky angler through the landing, a larger-than-usual swell rocked the *Lucy Sue*. As an experienced sailor, she had no trouble keeping her footing—but the fisherman in the stern didn't fare as well. He lost his balance, staggered toward the rail—and went into the drink headfirst.

Sweet heaven!

Never, in all her years of charter fishing, had she had a customer fall overboard.

As shock rippled through her, the guy's two companions reacted with hilarity. Hooting with laughter, they rose too and leaned over the edge of the boat.

"Hey, Marcus, you're not supposed to go in after the fish!" The sandy-haired guy continued to chortle.

A gust of wind whipped past, and the deck of the *Lucy Sue* tilted as another swell rolled by. Still laughing, the two guys staggered and grabbed the rail.

After snagging a life preserver, Kate elbowed them aside. Their friend was flailing in the water, bobbing up and down, and she heaved the preserver in his direction. "He's a good swimmer, right?" They'd all assured her they were.

"Yeah." The guy who responded swayed toward her and grinned. "In the country club pool, anyway."

As his breath hit her in the face, a chill ran up Kate's spine.

She didn't have much contact with alcohol, but the smell was distinctive.

Snatching up one of the almost empty water bottles, she sniffed. One whiff was all it took to confirm that the clear liquid inside wasn't H2O.

Her customers were drunk.

Anger bubbled up inside her, and every muscle in her body tensed. Alcohol and the sea didn't mix. Period. And she was always upfront about her no-alcohol rule with charter customers who booked trips.

But she hadn't mentioned it to these three. The trip had been impromptu, and she'd assumed their water bottles contained what the label indicated.

Big mistake.

Another swell rocked the boat—and as the college kids tottered again, panic washed over her. "You two, sit down! Now!"

"We can shee the fun better from here." The sandy-haired guy gave her a stupid grin.

She assessed their friend in the water. He was still floundering. Still trying without success to grasp the buoyant ring. If he was as drunk as his friends, he was in big trouble. The water was cold, the wind was rising and, in light of his inability to get a grip on the life preserver, the alcohol had significantly impaired his coordination.

Moving in close to the other two, Kate drew herself up to her full five-foot-three inches. Her short stature was no match for their six-foot-plus frames if they balked at her orders, but she knew how to take charge—and fear was a powerful motivator.

"Listen to me. I can get your friend back aboard. But if one of you falls in too, you could drown. That's what happens to drunk people in the water. They drown. Is this the day you want to die?" She enunciated each word.

The gravity of the situation seemed to register with the dark-haired customer.

"Come on, Stephen." He pulled his friend back from the railing and tried to push him into a chair.

"I wanna stay and watch the fun."

"Come on!" Pulling harder, he forced him down. Then he took his own seat.

That problem taken care of, Kate redirected her attention to the man overboard. He was treading water, but his efforts were slowing. If Chester was aboard, she could have had him maneuver the boat much closer to the victim while she shouted directions. As it was, she couldn't risk moving in too tight for fear of hitting him. And the two jerks sitting in the stern would be of no help in guiding her. For all she knew, they were seeing double.

The best she could do was try to position the boat a few feet away from the victim.

After accomplishing that maneuver as fast as possible, Kate put the engine in neutral and yanked a life jacket out of the bin. Slipped her arms through. Pulled the straps snug, struggling to stem her rising alarm as she kept tabs on Marcus. It was obvious he was tiring.

She unlatched the fish door in the stern and dropped to one knee.

"Marcus! Marcus, over here!" She waved her hands to catch his attention. "Grab the life preserver. It's to your left." If he could latch on to it, she could tow him back with the nylon rope that secured it to the boat.

He tried. But when she pulled on the rope he lost his grip…and disappeared under the gray swells.

Kate's heart stumbled.

When his head reappeared three seconds later, she'd already kicked off her shoes and slipped into the cold water.

The breath-stealing shock wasn't unexpected. The Nantucket sea was never warm, but in mid-May it still retained much of its winter chill. She had to move fast—before the numbing water impaired them both.

Striking out toward Marcus, she covered the distance in less than a dozen strokes and positioned herself out of arm's reach. He was a lot bigger than she was, and driven by panic-induced adrenaline, he could overwhelm her as he struggled to save himself.

She shoved the life preserver in his direction and tipped it up. "Put your arms through the hole."

Marcus lunged for the lifesaving doughnut. But he missed the hole, flipping it over—and away—instead.

Kate reached for it—and the thrashing kid locked onto her arm.

Shouldn't be a problem, though. If he couldn't hold on to the life preserver, there wasn't much chance he'd be able to hold on to her with one hand.

But as she prepared to yank free, his other arm swung around and landed a wild blow to the side of her face.

Searing pain radiated through her head, and she gasped as bright lights exploded behind her eyes, obscuring her vision.

Before she could regroup, Marcus climbed on top of her and shoved her face in the water, using her life-jacket-clad body to keep himself afloat.

Surrounded by blackness and locked in a death grip, Kate's tenuous hold on rational thought tottered as the danger slammed home.

She could die.

Right here.

Right now.

At the hands of a drunken college student, whose self-preservation instincts were about to cut her life short and rob Maddie of her mother.

No!

The silent, vehement denial ripped through Kate's mind.

She was *not* going to die!

Summoning up every ounce of her waning energy, Kate twisted and kicked and bucked.

At first her efforts had no effect. But just when her lungs felt ready to explode, she jabbed her elbow into Marcus's midsection with as much force as she could muster, loosening his grip enough to give her the opening she needed.

With a powerful shove, she kicked away from him and shot to the surface.

Sucking in air, Kate treaded water. Once she could breathe again, she retrieved the life preserver and moved back into position, ready to back off at the slightest indication Marcus was going to lunge for her again.

But he was spent. He was barely keeping his head above water now, and his pupils had gone glassy.

Time was running out.

She shoved the life preserver next to him and again tipped one end out of the water. "Marcus. Put your arms in the hole." She called out the instruction, speaking slowly.

She repeated the command once.

Twice.

On the third try, he managed to comply.

The first hurdle passed, Kate let the preserver drop back into the water, over his head. Snagging the attached nylon rope, she issued one more order as she prepared to tow him toward the *Lucy Sue.* "Hold on tight."

Buoyed by her life vest, Kate got him back to the boat with no problem. But hauling him through the fish door without assistance? Not happening. And he was in no shape to climb back on board himself.

Meaning one of his buddies was going to have to help her. Preferably the black-haired one, who seemed the least inebriated. What was his name again? Jack, that was it.

She hauled herself out of the water but remained on her

knees, issuing instructions over her shoulder as she reeled in Marcus. "Jack, tell Stephen to stay in his chair. Then get down on your hands and knees and come over here."

To her relief, the kid followed her orders. When he crawled up next to her, his pallor suggested that the gravity of the situation had finally registered in his alcohol-fogged brain.

"I want you to grab one of his hands. I'll grab the other. Stay off to the side of the fish door." The last thing she wanted was another headfirst tumble into the ocean. "On the count of three, pull."

Somehow, between the two of them, they managed to drag a spent Marcus back on deck, where he lay like an oversize bluefish—but with far less flopping about. Muscles quivering with fatigue, Kate closed the fish door. Another gust of wind ripped past under the graying sky, cutting through her sodden clothes and sending chills rippling through her.

Pushing past her exhaustion and bone-deep cold, Kate gripped the railing and pulled herself to her feet.

"I want everybody below. Jack, there are blankets down there. Do what you can to warm up Marcus. I'll get us back to the wharf as fast as I can."

After shepherding the trio into the cabin, Kate slipped her arms into her slicker and revved up the *Lucy Sue*'s engines. Turning hard to starboard, she pulled back on the throttle and set a straight course across Nantucket Sound, heading for the entrance to the harbor.

As the wind whipped past, bone-rattling shivers began to ripple through her, generated by cold, exposure, reaction—and a ton of anger.

Because of irresponsible behavior, lives could have been lost today—including hers.

And drowning at the hands of a drunk wasn't in her plans.

Yet the incident *had* been a reminder that God made the choices about when and how a life ended—and those choices didn't always mesh with human plans. He'd taken Mac in a way no one had expected…and far sooner than anyone would have chosen. Today, he could have called her home. Instead, she'd been spared. Perhaps because there was more he wanted her to do. More he wanted her to experience.

And maybe part of that more was Craig.

Maybe today's incident was a wake-up call. A reminder that fear and worry don't change the future. They only rob today of joy.

Brant Point Light and the Coast Guard station came into sight, and she pointed the *Lucy Sue* toward Straight Wharf.

If she let fear hold her back, she could avoid the pain of loss. But she would also eliminate the transforming grace of love that made life worth living. The kind of grace she'd known once, with Mac. And despite the hole his death had left in her life, if she had it to do again—knowing her days with him would be too few— she'd still marry him. He'd enriched her life in immeasurable ways.

As Craig could, if she gave him the opportunity.

She eased into her slip on Straight Wharf, fumbling with the lines as she secured them to the cleats on the pier—and reached a decision.

She was going to vanquish fear and remain open to the possibilities with Craig.

And as soon as she got out of these wet clothes, downed two aspirin to dull the throbbing pain on the right side of her face, and put ice on the eye that had swollen half shut during her enlightening ride home in the *Lucy Sue*, she intended to tell him that.

15

A s Craig exited the Hy-Line Cruises office after a meeting to discuss new passenger safety regulations, he paused to scan Straight Wharf. With the high season poised to begin in earnest, the slips were filling up and far more people were milling about than the day he'd first come down here a few weeks ago to tell Kate he was rescinding her safety citation.

Kate.

His lips flexed. If someone had told him three months ago he would end up falling in love with the red-haired spitfire who'd stormed into his office, he'd have laughed.

God, it seemed, had a sense of humor about such matters.

He started to turn away, but paused at a glimmer of red hair in the distance.

It was Kate, securing a line to her finger pier. She must have taken a spin in the *Lucy Sue.*

But why did the scene seem somehow…off?

He squinted at her as she straightened up, her movements stiff and jerky. And her hair was lank. No. Wait. It was wet. Not damp and frizzy wet from salt spray, but soaked through. As if she'd been caught in a downpour.

Except the dark clouds massing above hadn't yet released their rain.

That left only one other explanation for her drenched condition.

She'd taken an unplanned dip in the ocean.

And it wasn't likely she'd fallen overboard. Kate was experienced on the water. She was also careful. Besides, the sea was fairly placid, despite the ominous sky.

Could she have had another problem with the *Lucy Sue?*

All at once, she shifted her position, giving him a side view of her face.

Her black-and-blue face.

Pulse accelerating, Craig broke into a jog down Straight Wharf toward the *Lucy Sue*, keeping Kate in his sights. She motioned toward the cabin of her boat, and though he was too far away to hear what she was saying, the rigid profile of her jaw and her taut posture communicated anger.

A few moments later, three figures emerged onto the deck. Two were attired in shorts and T-shirts, while the third was wrapped in a blanket. They approached the stern, but Kate waved them back.

"Stay on deck until I have the boat secure! I'm not fishing anyone else out of the drink."

Mystery of her soaked condition solved.

But a dip in the sea to rescue someone who'd gone overboard didn't explain her bruises.

She turned toward him to secure the last line, and the closer-up view knotted his gut. Her right cheek was puffy and discolored, and her eye was swollen more than half shut.

Craig picked up his pace, arriving at the boat as she tightened her last knot and rose.

"Craig!" She took an involuntary step back, and he reached out to steady her. "What are you doing here?"

"I had business on Straight Wharf and I saw you in the distance. What's going on?" Without releasing her arm, he shot a narrow-eyed look at the three young men on the boat.

She shoved her wet hair back with a trembling hand. "These customers brought along bottles of water. Only it wasn't water. By the time I figured that out, they were drunk. One of them fell in. I had to go in after him."

"What happened to your face?"

"He tried to use me as a flotation device."

Enough said. Been there, done that as a rescue swimmer. Dealing with panicked people in the water was always dicey. Otherwise-loving husbands would almost drown their wives trying to stay afloat. Scrawny people developed superhuman strength when faced with their own demise. Adrenaline-fueled victims could cling with such ferocity that they'd put not only their life, but yours, in danger.

Perilous didn't come close to describing those scenarios. A terrorized person, no matter how puny, could sometimes overcome even a strong, well-trained swimmer.

And the guy with the blanket draped over him wasn't puny. Not by a long shot. Topping six feet, he had the build of an athlete.

In other words, he could have killed Kate.

Based on her tremors, she'd come to the same conclusion. And the cooling air and growing wind were only exacerbating her shakes.

Craig switched to official mode. "Do you have a change of clothes in the cabin?"

"Yes." Her teeth were beginning to chatter.

He stepped down into the boat and held out his hand. "Put them on."

"I can ch-change when I g-get home."

"You need to do it now, Kate. You know it's foolish to stay in wet clothes with the temperature dropping." He gentled his voice—but didn't back down.

Thankfully, she didn't argue. She placed her ice-cold hand in his and reboarded.

He waited until she pulled the cabin door shut behind her. Then, planting his fists on his hips, he leveled a cold, hard glare at the three offenders, blocking their exit.

"How old are you?"

"We're all over twenty-one." This from the dark-haired kid.

"Let me see your driver's licenses."

They fished them out, and Craig scanned the dates of birth. Too bad he couldn't get them for underage drinking. They were legal—barely. But they weren't going to walk away unscathed. Not after they'd hurt Kate. Not after what could have happened.

He pulled out a notebook and jotted down the information from their licenses. Then he folded his arms and pinned them with a blistering look until they squirmed and dropped their gazes.

"Let me tell you *boys* something. Alcohol and water don't mix. You"—he pointed to the kid draped in the blanket—"could be dead. So could the captain. Did you see her face? You hit her hard enough to knock her out. I don't think I have to tell you where you'd be if you had. As for you two"—he addressed the victim's buddies—"if Captain MacDonald had been overcome by your friend here, and you'd decided to play hero, trust me. All three of you would probably be fish bait."

The dark-haired kid swallowed. Hard. The middle one cringed. The one wearing the blanket blanched.

Point made.

"In case you boys don't know, I'm with the U.S. Coast Guard. We risk our lives every day to save people who get in trouble on the water. But we don't have a lot of patience for stupidity."

"We're really sorry about this, sir." The dark-haired kid again.

"We didn't mean to cause any problems. We were just celebrating the end of the semester and...well...I guess we got a little carried away." This from the guy in the blanket.

"We'll pay for any damages," the third one offered.

"Money doesn't fix everything." He folded his arms across his chest again. "But it will help with her medical expenses. Her next stop is the ER. I presume you boys will cover that."

"No problem," the dark-haired one said.

"I've got your addresses. Give me cell numbers."

Craig jotted them down as they complied, then jerked his head toward the pier. "I suggest you go home and sleep it off. And you"—he addressed the kid in the blanket, plucking it from around his shoulders as he spoke—"get out of those wet clothes. I assume I don't have to tell you not to drive."

"We walked down from the hotel."

"Smart move." Stepping aside, he allowed them to scramble out of the boat. They took off down the wharf at a trot.

After they disappeared from view, Craig grasped the rail with both hands, took several slow, deep breaths—and faced the truth.

Kate could have drowned today.

Just like Nicole and Aaron.

The very thing he'd convinced himself could never happen again had almost happened. History had come close to repeating itself.

His original instinct to avoid getting involved with a woman who made her living on the sea had been sound after all.

Now it was too late for second thoughts. She'd already invaded his life—and his heart.

But how was he supposed to deal with what had happened today?

"Craig?"

At the summons, he turned. Kate had emerged from the cabin, but she seemed shakier than ever as she clung to the edge of the door.

"I took a gander at my face in the mirror. I wish I hadn't." She tried to smile, but couldn't pull it off. "Wow! What a shiner."

Craig closed the distance between them, took her upper arms in a gentle grip, and angled her toward the light to inspect the bruises marring her creamy skin. "Are you hurt anywhere else?"

"No."

He ran his fingers lightly over the swelling on her cheek. "This needs medical attention."

"They're just bruises." She tried to pull away. "I'll heal."

He didn't relinquish his hold. "I'm taking you to the ER."

"No way."

"Come on, Kate. You could have damage to your eye. Or facial fractures. Did you black out?"

"No." Her breath hitched. "But I thought...he pushed my face in the water and...I know he was just scared...it wasn't intentional...but my lungs started to burn and...I kept thinking of Maddie." Her voice broke, and tears brimmed on her lower lashes. One spilled over, and she swiped it away as shudders rippled through her. "Sorry."

Despite his new doubts about their future, he pulled her close and tucked her against his chest, fingers tangling in her hair. "You're fine. It's over. Take a few deep breaths."

She clung to him, his shirt bunched in her fists, as she took one ragged breath after another until her respiration slowed and her shaking subsided. When at last she eased back, he let her go.

"Humor me on the trip to the ER, Kate."

"I can't. My last visit there with Maddie cost hundreds of dollars."

Of course money was why she'd balked. "You don't have to worry about that. Your customers are footing the bill."

Her eyebrows rose. "How did you manage that?"

"The uniform carries a certain intimidation factor—and I expect guilt played a role. As it should." A muscle in his jaw clenched as he regarded her battered face.

"In that case, I suppose it would be prudent to get checked out."

"The next order of business." Craig stepped onto the finger pier and extended his hand. She took it, grimacing as she transferred her weight from the boat to the wharf. "Are you sure you're not hurt anywhere else?"

"No. Just achy." She tucked her arm in his as they traversed Straight Wharf. "But as long as I can lean on you, I'll be fine."

Her comment jabbed him in the gut—and he gritted his teeth.

Yes, he could give her physical support to the ER.

But could he make the kind of emotional investment that could bankrupt his soul if he loved—and lost—again?

* * *

Two hours later, an ice pack from the ER pressed against her eye, Kate frowned as Craig walked her to her door.

Something was very wrong.

Despite his presence throughout the whole ER ordeal, he was distancing himself emotionally.

And it didn't take a genius to figure out why. He'd made no secret of his concerns about getting involved with a woman who earned her living on the sea. While those appeared to have subsided in the past few weeks, today they must have resurfaced with a vengeance.

How ironic was that?

The very event that had convinced her to move forward seemed to have sent him into retreat.

She fitted her key into the lock. "Thanks for sticking with me at the ER."

"No problem. Will you be all right here by yourself?"

"Yes. Edith is going to give Maddie dinner, so I don't even have to cook tonight. She's also close by if I need anything." Kate tucked the key back in her pocket and issued the invitation he'd no doubt turn down. "Would you like to come in?"

He hesitated, and she braced for his refusal. But he surprised her. "Just for a few minutes."

She twisted the knob and led the way inside. "Would you like a water or soda? I could also make coffee."

"No, thanks. Why don't we sit for a few minutes?" His tone was solemn. Weary.

She settled on the couch.

He chose a chair to the right.

Another negative omen.

She waited…but when the silence lengthened, she plunged in. "You're having second thoughts about us, aren't you? Because of what happened today."

He exhaled and wiped a hand down his face. "I was going to try to lead up to that with a bit more diplomacy."

"As you know, tact isn't my strong suit." Kate leaned forward, every muscle taut. The next few minutes would shape her future. "Here's the thing, Craig. I'm afraid of loss too. But despite my grief after Mac died, I wouldn't have wanted to miss one minute of my years with him. So even though relationships don't come with guarantees, I'm willing to explore ours. Because I don't want to spend the rest of my life alone—and lonely. Do you?"

Instead of answering, he rose and walked over to the French doors. Stared outside, where evening shadows had crept in, preventing the sunlight from penetrating the tall, thick privet hedge that insulated her yard from the world.

The predictable, steady tick of the antique clock on the mantel was the only sound in the tense silence as Kate prayed Craig would find the courage to let go of fear, as she had.

But when he turned and walked back, stopping behind the side chair, his bleak expression said her prayer had gone unanswered.

A little piece of her heart shriveled even before he spoke.

"I wish I could get past the fear, Kate. But I watched the sea claim one family. It almost took you today. And it could happen again." His voice choked, and he stopped. "You're out there every day. I don't know if I can live with that worry for the rest of my life."

She folded her hands, gripping them so tight her fingers ached. "Do you want me to promise never to set foot on a boat again? Is that what it would take to make this work?"

"I don't know what the answer is." He raked his fingers through his hair. "All I know is that just thinking about what might have happened today turns my blood to ice and twists my stomach into knots."

"And calling things off between us will make you happier?"

At her quiet question, a spasm contorted his features. "Not

in the short term—but it may be better for both of us long term."

"Better—or safer?"

"Maybe both. I just…I don't know."

Pressure built behind Kate's eyes. Every instinct in her body urged her to fight for this man. For them. To argue this out until he changed his mind.

But the decision to move forward had to come from him. From within. For now, all she could do was give him space—and hope he saw the light.

Heaviness weighing down her soul, she pushed herself to her feet. "I'll walk you to the door."

He followed, and as she reached for the knob his hand covered hers from behind.

"I'm sorry, Kate. I wish I knew how to get past the fear."

His breath was a whisper of warmth against her temple as he leaned close. Tempting her to push him into a decision he wasn't ready to make.

But was there anything wrong with reminding him what he'd be giving up if he walked away for always?

No.

Wiping her palms down her jeans, she pivoted, put her arms around his neck, rose on tiptoe—and moved in close.

His hands dropped to her waist. "Kate, I don't think—"

"Stop thinking." She tugged on his neck until he bent his head. Brushed her lips over his. Psyched herself up for rejection.

Instead, after a brief freeze, he drew her close and gave her exactly what she'd wanted.

The kiss of a lifetime.

Time passed. Or perhaps it stopped. Who knew?

When Craig eased back at last, his eyes had darkened to the

color of the sea at sunset on a cloudless summer day—and long-ing simmered in their depths. Fear might be holding him back, but the desire to move forward was there.

"You make it hard to walk away." His admission rasped.

"I'd rather you didn't."

The strong planes of his face flexed, as if his rigid self-con-trol had been pushed to the breaking point. "I have too many is-sues, Kate—and I don't want to let this go any further unless I can resolve them." His Adam's apple bobbed…and then he dropped his hands. Stepped back. "I'm sorry."

"I am too." She choked out her disappointment as she moved aside.

For a few seconds he hesitated. Then he walked out the door and closed it behind him with a gentle click, leaving her alone.

Perhaps for the rest of her life.

Unless she could come up with a way to alleviate his fears without abandoning the sea she loved.

16

Give it up, Cole. Now that the sun's risen, you're not going to go back to sleep. Besides, it's your mother's wedding day. Get up—and try to get in the spirit.

Yeah, yeah.

Heaving a sigh, he swung his legs to the floor. Stretched. Wandered over to the window.

For once, the meteorologists had gotten it right. The sky was clear, the winds were mild, the sun was bright. It would be a glorious day for a wedding.

Too bad he wasn't in the mood.

But the past ten days had been the longest of his life, and sleep had been elusive—leaving him exhausted and on edge.

Not that anyone had noticed. He'd gone through the motions at work. Paid special attention to Vicki. Conferred with Edith as his mother's wedding plans were finalized.

Only his mom had picked up on his funk with her usual keen intuition. Though he'd declined her if-there's-anything-you'd-like-to-talk-about-I'm-available offer, the truth was he could use an empathetic ear.

Not today, though.

Today all the attention should be on his mom.

After taking a quick shower and donning casual attire, he wandered into the kitchen.

To his surprise, his mother was already at the table, eating an English muffin.

"Too nervous to sleep?" He hiked up one side of his mouth as he poured himself a cup of coffee.

"I slept like a baby. You're the one who looks like you could use a decent night's sleep."

"I have a lot on my mind." He leaned back against the counter and sipped the strong brew.

"It can't have anything to do with Vicki. She's flourishing. You've done a fine job with her."

"Thanks. Having a friend her own age helped."

"I agree. Edith told me all about Maddie. I met that little charmer and her mother yesterday when we settled Harold into the guest cottage behind Edith's house. Or Honeymoon Central, as Harold's calling it." She waggled her eyebrows, a roguish spark glinting in her irises. "Anyway, I liked Kate. Edith said the two of you are friends."

Pushing off from the counter, Craig stuck his head in the refrigerator on the pretext of searching for the orange juice. No surprise that his mother had gotten an earful from Edith. The two of them had become friends during the past few weeks as they'd consulted on the wedding. "I see her on a regular basis since Edith watches both girls."

"Hmm." She nibbled at her muffin. "Heather at The Devon Rose said she could accommodate one or two more people for the reception. She's used to serving afternoon tea for much larger groups. Would you like to reconsider inviting Kate and her daughter?"

"No."

She added another splash of cream to her coffee, stirring it until the dark liquid was diluted to the color of rich mocha. "You know, guilt and fear can be very debilitating."

They were approaching restricted territory. "Kind of a heavy subject for so early in the morning—and on such a special day. Let's talk about you."

"I *was* talking about me. Who did you think I was talking about?" She gave him a shrewd appraisal.

Blast.

He'd walked right into that one.

Ignoring her question, he took a seat at the table. "What do you have to feel guilty about?"

"Your dad's death."

Craig blinked. "What are you talking about?"

She picked at her half-eaten muffin. "I never told you boys this, but I always believed it was my fault he died."

"That's ridiculous! He had a heart attack."

"Shoveling snow. He was too old for that, son. But I was more worried about my bridge club ladies falling than I was about his heart. I should have paid the kid up the block to do it."

"No one could have predicted that heart attack, Mom. And Dad liked to take care of maintenance himself."

"I know. I finally made peace with that." She wiped a speck of jam off the table. "But I also felt guilty about falling in love again. Plus, it almost killed me when your dad died. I wasn't certain I could risk that kind of loss again. After bending the Lord's ear about it, though, I came to several conclusions. No one is perfect. No one can control everything. And fear not only locks us in the past, it denies us a future."

He wrapped his fingers around the mug, letting the warmth seep into his cold fingers. "Sounds like you've thought this through."

"I have. Long and hard." She pushed aside her muffin and touched his hand. "I don't know what regrets you harbor, or what fears are holding you back, Craig. But if I can learn to let mine go and move on at seventy, you can do it at thirty-nine." She rose. "And now I have a wedding to get ready for."

She disappeared down the hall...but long after she left, the hard-won wisdom she'd imparted continued to loop through his mind.

And plant a tiny seed of hope.

* * *

Six hours later, in a simple but touching ceremony under a cloudless sky, Craig watched as Lillian Cole became Mrs. Harold Simmons in front of a small group of family and new friends.

His brother, Steve, stood beside Harold as best man, while Steve's wife, teenage son, and preteen daughter clustered nearby. The groom's daughter flanked Lillian as matron of honor, her husband and three boys a few feet away. Vicki, in a white dress with a pink sash, stayed close to Lillian as the flower girl. Edith and Chester had linked arms.

Only he stood alone.

By choice.

But since his mother's confession this morning, the choice that had appeared to be prudent didn't seem as cut-and-dried anymore.

Less so after Reverend Kaizer commended Lillian and Harold for having the courage to begin a journey together at an age many considered too late for new beginnings, then pointed out that, as Mark wrote in scripture, all things are possible with God.

And it was further undermined at The Devon Rose as he watched Edith and Chester share a private laugh in one corner...as Harold's daughter and son-in-law gathered their children

together for a family photo…and as his brother's family entertained Vicki, who was enjoying being the center of attention
while Lillian and Harold stepped into the garden for a few more
pictures.

Vicki skipped over, followed by the eleven-year-old cousin
she barely remembered from the whirlwind stop his brother's
family had made in Washington last year on their way home from
a vacation in South Carolina.

"Daddy, can I go with Lauren to their beach house?"

"I'll take care of her, Uncle Craig." Lauren put a protective
arm around her shoulders.

"We all will." Steve joined the group. "It would be a great
opportunity for the cousins to get reacquainted. Why don't you
come too? I know we're all getting together for dinner tomorrow
night, but we could extend the party for a while today. It's still
early."

Given his unsettled emotional state, socializing held zero appeal.

"I have to stop by the station and see what's going on." Not
required, but it was the first excuse that came to mind.

"Maybe after that?"

"Depending on what I find, that's a possibility." But one that
wasn't going to pan out. There was always paperwork waiting to
be reviewed.

"In the meantime, can we take Vicki?" Steve bent down and
tugged one of the little girl's pixie locks, making her giggle. "An
uncle shouldn't be denied a visit with his only niece."

"Fine with me. I'll stop by later to pick her up if I can't get
away sooner."

Not long after, the party broke up and the newlyweds departed in a shower of birdseed to Edith's cottage—aka

Honeymoon Central.

After a quick stop at the station, Craig made the short, solitary drive home, trading his uniform for jeans and a cotton shirt as he glanced at the photo of him and Kate and Vicki and Maddie.

They looked like a family.

That was an illusion.

But it could be real someday—if he could find the courage to put his fears to rest, as Kate had. As his mother had.

And if he couldn't?

The bleakness that had returned in the ten days since he'd broken up with Kate would forever dim his world.

What an ulcer-inducing dilemma.

And pacing in the small room wasn't helping matters. What he needed was fresh air. Open space. Wide vistas.

He snatched his keys off the dresser and strode toward the garage.

Only one place could give him what he craved. The place where his thoughts were always clearer. Where he most often felt the presence of God.

He needed the sea.

Ten minutes later, Craig stepped onto Dionis Beach, took a cleansing breath of the salt air, and scanned the deserted expanse of sand.

No. Scratch that. It wasn't deserted. In the distance, a lone figure sat close to the water.

A lone *red-haired* figure.

Kate.

He gaped at her.

What were the odds she'd choose this time, this place, for contemplation, as he had?

Was it coincidence—or something more?

And if it was something more, why was he fighting it so hard? Kate had battled fears and reservations too—but she'd made her peace with them. Why couldn't he?

As he traced her slim profile and watched the wind toss her flyaway hair, the words she'd said the night of the accident replayed in his mind.

Even though relationships don't come with guarantees, I'm willing to explore ours. Because I don't want to spend the rest of my life alone—and lonely. Do you?

Standing here in the ebbing daylight, as sea and sky darkened, the answer crystalized.

No. He didn't.

The last ten days had slammed that home. Without Kate to chase away the shadows, his life had been dim and dreary. She'd flipped on the light for him, just as Harold had done for his mother.

And like it or not, the simple truth was she'd staked a claim on his heart. Even if he walked away forever, Kate MacDonald would always be part of him—and he'd feel her loss as keenly as if death, rather than fear, had robbed him of her presence.

His mother, in her typical wisdom, had been right. If he let it, fear would deny him the future that beckoned. A future filled with joy and light and hope.

All at once, a burden lifted from his shoulders. For while his fears hadn't evaporated, they'd lost the power to control his life.

Spirits soaring, Craig strode across the sand toward the woman who'd claimed his heart with her strength and kindness and courage and a dozen other endearing qualities.

He stopped a few feet away. "Hello, Kate."

She jerked and swung around. "Craig! What are you doing

here?"

"Thinking about us." He dropped down beside her, drawing up his legs and clasping his hands between his knees. "What are *you* doing here?"

"The same. Where's Vicki?"

"With my brother. Where's Maddie?"

"With Edith. I heard the wedding was lovely."

"It was. Edith is quite the organizer."

"Trust me. I know." Kate's lips curved into a quick rueful smile, then flattened. "I was going to call you after the wedding excitement died down. I've been thinking and praying over the past ten days, and I have a proposition for you. I can't promise never to set foot on a boat again. The sea is in my blood, and it will always be part of my life. But if my job is the deal-breaker, I can sell the *Lucy Sue* and teach full-time. Because if I have to choose between making a living on the sea or giving up on our relationship, I choose us."

As he gazed at her, pressure built in his throat.

Sweet heaven, how he loved this woman! More than ever for her willingness to forfeit something so important to her in order to give them a chance.

But that was a sacrifice she didn't have to make.

Twining his fingers with hers, he angled toward her. "I would never ask you to do that, Kate. I wouldn't want to change one aspect of who you are, and that"—he swept his hand over the expanse of sea—"is as much a part of you as it is a part of me."

"You didn't ask. I offered."

"I know—and I can't even put into words how much that means to me. But I've been thinking and praying too...and I've come to accept that life doesn't have guarantees. All I can do is be grateful for the blessings of today—because no one is promised tomorrow. And one of those blessings is you." He reached over. Touched a springy curl that refused to be restrained.

Like the woman herself, who'd battled challenges that would have defeated a lesser person.

Kate drew in a long, unsteady breath, and her emerald irises began to shimmer. "Are you certain about this?"

"Yes." He played with her hair, winding his finger in a fiery lock. "And if everything goes the way I hope it will, you may find yourself with a new first mate. In life, and on the *Lucy Sue*— after this Coast Guard lieutenant retires. What do you say?"

Joy chased the last vestige of tension from her features as she grinned, scooted closer, and threw her arms around his neck.

"I say let's open up the throttle and let 'er rip."

Epilogue

Had there ever been such a glorious October day?

Kate rested her elbow on the open window of her car and inhaled the unseasonable balmy air as she followed Polpis Road past the Lifesaving Museum and through the moors and bogs. Life was good—and getting better every day, thanks to the extraordinary man who'd stolen her heart, filled her world with joy, and added sparkle to her days.

Like today.

A tingle of anticipation zipped through her. Thanks to Craig's string-pulling, she was about to get a rare inside peek at the iconic Sankaty Head Light that had been moved hundreds of feet from its perch on the edge of a steep and eroding cliff a few years before—a feat that remained a subject of discussion among Nantucketers.

It had been a no-brainer to drop everything when he'd called earlier, after she'd arrived home from subbing, to ask if she could meet him. Edith, bless her heart, had been happy to keep Maddie for an extra hour.

She parked beside the chained-off maintenance road that led to the lighthouse, next to Craig's car, and trekked down the gravel track. Some sort of official business must have prompted his trip out here, since the Coast Guard managed all of the island's lighthouses.

A handwritten note was attached to the door at the base of the tower, and she stopped to read it.

I'm at the top, Kate. Come on up. Craig.

Strange that he hadn't waited for her at the bottom, but hey. As long as she got to peek inside, no worries.

She stepped into the murky space. While the outside of the tower was painted white with a broad red horizontal stripe around the middle, the interior featured exposed brick. An intimidating, wire-mesh spiral staircase wound upward—but she hadn't come this far to chicken out.

Gripping the handrail, Kate began the long ascent.

As she approached the lantern room at the top, puffing a bit after the dizzying vertical climb, she tipped her head back. The floor of the landing below the lantern room was visible now.

"Craig?"

"I'm at the top, Kate." His deep voice echoed through the cavernous tower, but he remained out of sight.

She continued to ascend until the spiral stairs deposited her on the landing, near the metal ladder that provided access to the lantern room.

Metal ladder, hmm?

Lucky she'd worn an old pair of jeans for this adventure.

She gripped the rungs and climbed the last few feet.

As her head emerged through the opening in the floor, a blue-coated arm reached down. After taking her hand in a firm grip, Craig helped her up the final rungs.

"Welcome to the top of the world."

Any other time, the breathtaking view from the eight-sided glass enclosure housing the huge lens that flashed every seven and a half seconds would have claimed her full attention. But at that moment, she only had eyes for the man whose warm, intimate smile set her pulse racing. And the full dress uniform only added to his appeal.

"Wow." She gave him an appreciative scan. "Big meeting today?"

"Huge."

He pulled out his cell. Pressed a button.

Strains of Vivaldi filled the small room.

Then he bent down and reached behind her. When he straightened up, he was holding a spray of red roses—which he extended to her. "For you."

"Wow again." Her heart did a flip-flop as she took the flowers, lifted the velvet petals toward her face, and inhaled the heady scent. Music, flowers, a spectacular setting—it could mean only one thing.

She hoped.

Because she was more than ready to commit forever to the man who'd stolen her heart—and filled it with dreams.

* * *

She seemed pleased by his romantic gesture. And receptive.

A positive sign.

He hoped.

Craig swallowed, fighting back a case of nerves far worse than any he'd ever experienced on a life-or-death rescue mission.

Probably because his life—and the way it would play out in the years to come—hung in the balance.

"I have a feeling you know where this is leading."

"I could make a guess. This"—she swept a hand over the setting—"is very romantic."

"After hearing about the fabulous birthdays Mac planned for

you, I wanted to do this right."

"I would never compare the two of you. Your gifts are uniquely yours." She touched his cheek, her eyes alight with love.

That was encouraging.

"Still, I wanted you to remember this moment for the rest of your life."

"Done." She lifted the roses to inhale again the sweet scent that was perfuming the small, intimate space—and gave him a cheeky grin. "Is there a speech to go with this?"

"Yes." He took a deep breath and wove his fingers through hers. "Three years ago, I thought my world had ended. I lost my faith and my love of the sea—and I almost lost touch with my daughter. Then I met you, and like this light that guides lost souls home"—he nodded toward the lens—"you illuminated my life and helped me start down a new path. One I'd like to travel with you every day for the rest of my life. Katherine MacDonald, would you do me the honor of becoming my wife?"

Her eyes began to glisten. "You sure know how to stage a proposal, Lieutenant."

"Is that a yes?"

"That is most definitely a yes."

Thank you, Lord!

Craig took the flowers, set them aside, and tenderly cupped her face with his hands. "I love you, Kate." A tremor threaded through his voice.

"I love you too." She put her arms around his neck and lifted her chin. "I think there's one more step to make this official."

He gave a quiet chuckle. "Why do I think communication will never be a problem in our relationship?"

"No worries on that score. You're engaged to a strong-willed woman who isn't afraid to ask for what she wants."

"I learned that the day we met. But sometimes words aren't necessary. What do you say we try out some nonverbal communication?"

"Count me in." She snuggled closer. "Let the adventure begin."

He didn't hesitate to lower his head and claim her lips.

Because life with Kate would, indeed, be one grand adventure.

Starting now.

And as she gave a soft sigh...as her fresh scent invaded his pores...as the setting sun burnished her springy curls...Craig gave thanks.

For though it hadn't seemed so at the time, God had smiled on him the day Katherine MacDonald stormed into his office. She'd rocked his world, shaken his resolutions, forced him to face tough questions.

But she'd also given him the courage to move on. To reconnect with his daughter. To believe, as Reverend Kaizer had said at his mother's wedding, that all things are possible with God.

Most of all, she'd given him a beacon of hope that was as steady and sure as the tides. For with her strength, her candor, her deep capacity to love, she'd turned on the light in his life.

And because of her, all his tomorrows would be lived in sunlight rather than shadows.

Keep reading for a preview of Book 2!

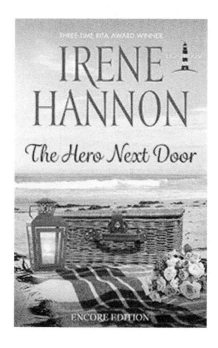

~Excerpt~

The Hero Next Door

LIGHTHOUSE LANE—BOOK 2
ENCORE EDITION

1

Let the healing begin.

As the Hyannis ferry churned into Nantucket Harbor, Justin Clay filled his lungs with the salt air on this sunny first day of June—and the first day of a new chapter in his life.

He hoped.

Forearms resting on the railing, he took in the view as the ferry rounded diminutive Brant Point Light and the Coast Guard station. Boats of every type and size dotted the blue water below the tree-filled town that perched on a gentle hillside in the background. The gold dome of a clock tower and a tall white steeple soared over the leafy branches, while weathered gray clapboard buildings with white trim predominated along the waterfront.

Justin lifted his face to the sun, letting the warm rays seep into his pores. He'd wanted a complete change of scene, and this fit the bill. The tranquil, pristine vista felt a world removed from the violent, gritty backstreets of Chicago. Perhaps here, twenty-six miles from the mainland, on this fourteen-by-three-and-a-half-mile speck of land in the Atlantic Ocean, he would find release from the pain and guilt that gnawed at his soul.

As the ferry eased beside the wharf, he picked up his over-size duffel bag and slung his backpack over one shoulder. Not much luggage for a three-month stay—but if his prayers were answered, he'd be leaving most of his baggage behind when he reboarded the ferry in twelve weeks and set sail for home.

* * *

Sliding a tray of mini-scones onto the cooling rack on the stain-less-steel prep table, Heather Anderson checked the clock. 1:10 p.m. In less than an hour, thirty-four customers would be arriving for a proper British afternoon tea.

Where was Julie?

As she flicked a glance out the window, the gate by the gar-age swung open to admit her assistant. Thank goodness. The Devon Rose could function as a one-woman show for most of the day, but attending to customers required two people.

Julie pushed through the back door, her white blouse and black skirt immaculate even if her French braid was slightly askew. "Sorry. I had a flat tire."

"No worries." Heather adjusted the oven temperature, strode over to the commercial-size refrigerator, and pulled out a tray of mini-quiches. "Did Todd change it for you?"

"Yes—but I hated to wake him." Julie began arranging the scones on the second level of the three-tiered silver serving stands lined up on the counter, tucking flowers among them. "There was a drug incident in the wee hours of the morning, and he was beat when he got home. But he didn't complain about the tire."

"And you've been married to that cop for how long? Twenty

years?" Heather shook her head as she took the lids off fifteen teapots in a variety of styles and arranged them on a long counter. "He's one in a million. Count your blessings."

"I do. Every day. But there are other good guys out there too, you know." She paused in her tray-filling task for emphasis.

"Maybe." Heather slid the quiches into the oven. "But they're few and far between. And given past experience, not likely to come calling at my door. I'd have to beat the bushes to find one." She closed the oven door and turned to Julie. "And as far as I'm concerned, it's not worth the effort."

End of story.

* * *

Justin hoisted his backpack into a more comfortable position, pulled the Nantucket town map out of the back pocket of his jeans, and perused the maze of streets. In one more block he'd be at Lighthouse Lane—and the cottage he'd be calling home for the next three months.

After refolding the map, he shoved it back into his pocket, hefted his duffel bag, and continued down the sidewalk. Unlike the dirty, decaying back alleys of Chicago, Nantucket was clean and well kept. And the people he'd passed, many on bicycles, had offered pleasant greetings—a welcome change from the suspicious looks he usually got, cast by questionable characters as they slunk into dark doorways.

Nantucket wasn't crime free. No place was. But it was doubtful he'd have to worry about double-crosses here—or mistakes that could snuff out lives.

Pausing at the corner of Lighthouse Lane, he swallowed past the bitter taste in his mouth. Maybe coming to Nantucket hadn't been such a hot idea, after all. Maybe he should have used the last three months of his four-month leave to veg. Rent a cabin in the woods and disappear. Or borrow a boat and hang out on Lake Michigan.

Yet this summer job opportunity...a chance to return to his roots as a beat cop...had seemed providential.

And it was too late for second thoughts anyway.

Putting his feet back in gear, he crossed the street and turned left onto Lighthouse Lane. According to his landlady, Edith Shaw, hers was the third—and last—house on the right...and the Federal-style home was easy to spot.

But far more impressive was the two-story structure on the corner. Constructed of clapboard like the Shaw house, but painted white instead of yellow, it featured black shutters. A Greek Revival roofline with a deep frieze—along with a small, elevated, white-pillared front porch—gave it a grand, stately air. A discreet sign beside the door identified it as The Devon Rose.

Squinting, he read the elaborate script below the name: *Serving Wednesday through Sunday.*

Sounded like a restaurant—and mere steps away from his new digs. Sweet. Once he dropped his bags off at the cottage, he could come back here for a quick bite to tide him over until he stocked his kitchen.

Taking the cue from his grumbling stomach, he picked up his pace, passing a snug, weathered clapboard cottage with sage-colored trim that was sandwiched on a shallow lot between The Devon Rose and the Shaw house. Meaning the backyards of the two larger houses adjoined in the rear.

At Edith's house, he found an envelope bearing his name taped beside the doorbell. The note inside directed him through the half-moon gate in the tall privet hedge to a spacious private backyard. From there he followed a flagstone path across the thick carpet of grass to the cottage, which was surrounded by budding hydrangea bushes. It was tucked into the back corner, separated from The Devon Rose property only by the hedge.

The structure was small—as he'd been warned—but square footage wasn't an issue. Headroom, however, mattered for a six-foot-one frame. Hopefully the compact accommodations wouldn't be too claustrophobic.

That fear was put to rest the instant he stepped through the door, thanks to the vaulted ceiling. A queen-size bed stood in the far left corner of the room, while a small couch upholstered in hydrangea-print fabric hugged the wall to the left of the front door, a brass reading lamp beside it. An old chest, topped with a glass bowl of hard candy, served as a coffee table. In the tiny kitchenette to the right, a wooden café table was flanked by matching chairs with blue-and-yellow plaid seat cushions.

A quick peek confirmed that the bath was behind the kitchen. No tub, but a decent-size shower.

Not bad digs to call home for the next three months.

As he set his luggage on the polished pine floor, he eyed a plate of what appeared to be homemade pumpkin bread in the middle of the café table.

At another prompt from his stomach, he stripped off the plastic wrap and devoured one of the slices. But it barely put a dent in his appetite.

He needed real food.

After rewrapping the plate of sweet bread, he freshened up and headed back out the door to the closest restaurant.

The Devon Rose.

About the Author

© DeWeesePhotography.com

Irene Hannon is the bestselling, award-winning author of more than sixty contemporary romance and romantic suspense novels. She is also a three-time winner of the RITA Award—the "Oscar" of romance fiction—from Romance Writers of America, and a member of that organization's elite Hall of Fame.

Her many other awards include National Readers' Choice, Daphne du Maurier, Retailers' Choice, Booksellers' Best, Carol, and Reviewer's Choice from *RT Book Reviews* magazine, which also honored her with a Career Achievement Award for her entire body of work. In addition, she is a two-time Christy Award finalist.

Millions of copies of her books have been sold worldwide, and her novels have been translated into multiple languages.

Irene, who holds a BA in psychology and an MA in journalism, juggled two careers for many years until she gave up her executive corporate communications position with a Fortune 500 company to write full-time. She is happy to say she has no regrets.

A trained vocalist, Irene has sung the leading role in numerous community musical theater productions and is a soloist at her church. She and her husband enjoy traveling, hiking, Saturday mornings at their favorite coffee shop, and spending time with family. They make their home in Missouri.

To learn more about Irene and her books, visit www.irenehannon.com. She loves to interact with readers on Facebook, and is also active on Twitter and Instagram.

Printed in Great Britain
by Amazon

40260682R00128